Something is going on!

Haunts and Spirits of the Past

Colonel Charles Dahnmon Whitt

ISBN 978-1-931672-71-9
Dahnmon Whitt Family
In cooperation with Jesse Stuart Foundation
Ashland Kentucky

First Edition January 17, 2011

Copyright 2010 by Colonel Charles Dahnmon Whitt

All rights reserved. NO part of this book may be reproduced or utilized in any form or by any means without the permission from the publisher.

Published by:

Jesse Stuart Foundation
1645 Winchester Avenue, Ashland, Kentucky 41101
dahnmonwhittfamily.com

Contents

Spiritual Power of Tecumseh

Source: the book, "The Patriot, Hezekiah Whitt"

Governor William Henry Harrison sat down and wrote a letter late in July 1811 to Secretary of War Eustis describing the last meeting and the man, Tecumseh.

The implicit obedience and respect which the followers of Tecumseh pay him are wonderful. If it were not the vicinity of the United States, he would perhaps be the founder of an empire that would rival in glory Mexico or Peru. No difficulties deter him. For four years he has been in constant motion. You see him today on the Wabash, and in a short time hear of him on the shores of Lake Erie or Michigan, or on the banks of the Mississippi; and wherever he goes he makes an impression favorable to his purpose. He is now upon the last round to put a finishing stroke to his work. I hope, however, before his return that part of the work which he considered complete will be demolished, and even its foundation rooted up.

I remain, Sir, Your Most Obedient Servant,
William Henry Harrison

Tecumseh took bundles of red sticks and gave some to each tribe he visited.

Back before the bundles were large, but now they were getting smaller.
Tecumseh was led by the Great Spirit and this was a sign of things to come. Among some of his greater predictions were a total eclipse of the Sun and the sighting of a Comet. The next to come would be the greatest.

He had gained fame with the Cherokee, Seminoles, Lower Creeks, the Santee's, Catawba's, Choctaws Biloxi's, Chickasaws, Alabama's, and the Mobiles as he gave them a bundle of red sticks. Some tribes wanted a sign now and he always came up with one. The Seminoles doubted him and he told them to go to the sea at a certain point on the Florida coast and they would receive guns and power from a ship. They went and a British ship was waiting for them and gave them what they wanted. They were believers now.

Next Tecumseh headed to the land across the Mississippi to visit the Upper Creeks, Natchez, Caddos, Tawakiois, and Yazoo and more. Those that had doubts of this Shawnee chief he would tell them of the great sign. He told them when he got back to the north and each red stick had been burned watch and listen. He would stomp his foot and their houses would fall. This will be the time to come and join the whole Indian Nation.

Back at Tippecanoe half a dozen warriors, of several tribes, bent on mischief came and ask the *(Prophet, Tenskwatawa, The ambitious brother of Tecumseh in which Tecumseh confided and gave him small predictions was in charge while Tecumseh was away recruiting tribes for his Confederacy.)* if they could sneak down to Vincennes and steal a horse apiece undetected. All the tribes had learned to work together. Tenskwatawa knew better, but he let them go as if it was his idea.

The Indians returned in a few days with their horses and bragging about the affray. Next day rode in fifteen armed white men whom had followed the horse prints to Tippecanoe. They rode in and spoke to the Prophet demanding the horses be returned.

Tenskwatawa laughed it off as if saying boys will be boys, but the soldiers didn't think it was funny. They took the horses and headed back down the Wabash.

Tenskwatawa went to his wegiwa (Shawnee word for dwelling.) to think about what happened and came out in a short time. He called the people together and told them he had a vision. The vision was for him to send a large group of warriors to intercept the whites and get the horses back. He told them none would be harmed and that the horses were theirs. In a short time about fifty warriors thundered out after the horses the whites had come and taken.

The warriors came up on the fifteen white men at their night camp and rode right in. They took the six and also the fifteen horses the white men rode. They set the whites to foot and told them to never come back to Tippecanoe.

William Henry Harrison waited for such an excuse as this and Tecumseh was not at home. In three weeks Harrison was leading his 900 man army toward Tippecanoe.

Tenskwatawa worked the Indians into a frenzy and they were ready for a fight. Tenskwatawa had told the warriors that the white man's bullets would not strike them. The plan was drawn up that the chiefs of the different tribes would go and talk to the Governor whom now had his army stationed on a nearby hill. The chiefs would make any concession the Governor demanded and leave except for two. The two lingering chiefs were to yank out their pistols and kill William Henry Harrison and this would start the battle.

During the dark night Tenskwatawa danced around as if in a trance and acted as if the Great Spirit had his mind. He came abruptly back to himself and said that half the white soldiers are crazy and the other half are dead. You need only to go in and finish them off with tomahawks.

Tenskwatawa couldn't wait until the daylight. He sent them, at least 1000 painted warriors, to attack the Shemanese. (White Soldiers) It was around 4:00 AM on November 7, 1811 and Harrison was putting on his boots to call the men to rise. A shot rang out and a soldier shot an Indian that was sneaking up on him. The soldiers had slept with their muskets in their hands and rose quickly. The fires were put out and the battle was on. They fought in darkness as they tried to determine who was friend or foe. Screams and gun blasts disturbed the quiet night. Even the hacking and slamming of war clubs and tomahawks made the eerie sounds of bones crushing.

The Governor jumped on his horse and rode from one place to another directing his men. He rode to the hottest places of the battle and had his hair parted by a ball which went through the brim of his hat, but no ball hit him anywhere else. His bravery stopped a clear victory by the Indians.

Tenskwatawa stood on a hill, out of range of the battle, danced, chanted, and screamed encouragement to the warriors. He had it in his mind that the warriors were winning a great battle. Some of the Indians ran to Tenskwatawa and told him that the bullets were indeed killing the warriors. He just kept chanting and urged the warriors to fight on. Tenskwatawa screamed louder even then the gunshots and screams of battle. The Indians believed the Great Spirit was protecting them and rushed right into awaiting bayonets. In the gray dawn it became so apparently clear that the Great Spirit was not helping the red warriors. The Indians regained their wisdom and disappeared into the nearby woods.

After the battle 188 bodies laid all about. Only 38 were Indians, yet it was a victory for Harrison and his army. Tenskwatawa had undone many years of work by Tecumseh in only one night. The battle was over and Tecumseh would be enraged to the point of murder when he would hear the news. The news of the victory would spread like wild fire to the east and south. Now what tribe could put confidence in the brothers, Tenskwatawa and Tecumseh?

Kentucky, Ohio, Pennsylvania, and Virginia would be pleased to hear of the great victory.

Tecumseh Stomps His Foot

He sends a powerful sign to his Native Americans and to the Whites.

Back on Tippecanoe River it was as if a bomb had gone off. The Indians saw that the Prophet had no real power and they scattered. A strong group of the Indians that were loyal to Tecumseh started a new village on Wildcat Creek. In the center of the new town was an ugly little Indian tied to a pole, it was the Prophet, Tenskwatawa.

The old village was pillaged by Harrison's army and burned. They found cases of brand new muskets that had been given by the British. There was nothing left of "Prophet Town".

Cheers went up as a party of Indians entered the town on Wildcat Creek. It was their beloved leader, Tecumseh and his faithful braves. Tecumseh stopped his horse abruptly and dismounted. His hardened eyes had spotted his brother. Tenskwatawa had hoped that Tecumseh would take pity on him, but his hope was dashed as he saw his livid brother walking toward him with a big skinning knife in his hand.

Tecumseh jerked Tenskwatawa's head around by gripping his hair. He laid the sharp blade to his exposed neck and pulled it slightly and drew a trickle of blood that slowly moved down to the base of his neck. Tenskwatawa thought he was dead for sure! Tecumseh shoved him to the ground and stood to face his friends that had saved a remnant of his Confederation.

Death for the Prophet was too good, in a single day he had destroyed ten years of work. He had caused pain and coming destruction to all Indians as the great plan was all but broken. Tecumseh cast his brother out to be scorned. He was no longer the Prophet, not a brother, not an Indian, not even a man. Tenskwatawa would have neither family nor people; he would die a little each day until the demons of the underworld came for him.

Tecumseh would have to go to plan "B" and he hated it so badly. He would have to join the British against the seventeen fires (Shawnee description of the seventeen states.). Tecumseh believed that many of the brave warriors that had lost hope could be brought back.

Tecumseh was still guided by the Great Spirit. There would be a sign in the night sky; a great Comet of greenish light had passed through the sky (Remember that Tecumseh's name means panther crossing the sky as a comet did cross the sky the night the great man was born.) Now after the tribes took the last red stick that had been given to almost all the tribes in two thirds of what is now the United States. They cut it into thirty pieces as instructed by the great Tecumseh. A piece was burned each morning, now all was gone and the tribes would not have a fire until the great sign came. Indians to the far north, to the south to Florida, to the west beyond the Dakotas sat in the last night with no fire and waited. Of course the northern tribes were wrapped in blankets to ward off the winter cold. (Some of the tribes became known as the red stick people.)

On December 16, 1811 at about 2:30 AM, Tecumseh stomped his foot! The whole eastern half of the land now called the United States shook as if the Great Spirit was venting his anger. Tremors were felt all over America and it is still considered to be the strongest earthquake in history.

Creeks and lakes empted out and formed new paths and lakes, trees fell all over the land, huge boulders rolled down the mountains from Florida to way up in Canada. Reel Foot Lake on the Kentucky-Tennessee border was not a lake until on that faithful day when the earth shook so violently that millions of gallons of water spring up from the earth to form it. It is still there today. The Great Lakes churned with huge waves that came up over the highest banks. It shook as far as Yellowstone to the west. (Anvil Rock in Greenup County, Kentucky is documented as proof of this great sign. It lies at the foot of a hill near Lloyd, Kentucky to this day after rolling off the ridge above it.)

Wild animals and birds were scared from their beds and roosts, cattle in the fields fell to the ground. There was no doubt as to this great sign predicted by the great Chief Tecumseh. The center of the quake was near New Madrid, Missouri and is thought to be an 8 plus on the rector scale. This quake happened where there had never been one recorded before; no scientific explanation could be given. Only that the Great Tecumseh had stomped his foot.

There is no record to the lives lost or property destroyed, but if it happened today the cost may have been one million lives and billions of dollars lost in property. Memphis Tennessee would be leveled. Back in Tazewell County, Virginia many folks were shaken out of their beds and any weak structures hit the ground. Many rock houses in the cliffs of the mountains collapsed and some think that Swift's Silver Mine vanished this way.

The Whitts were up and quiet alarmed. Rachel, (Wife of Hezekiah Whitt and the daughter of the Great Chief Cornstalk.) spoke quietly to Hezekiah, trying not to scare the others in the house.

"It's Tecumseh's sign," she said.

Even Hezekiah knew something super natural was going on, could it be from God or could it be evil power from the devil?

The shaking on December 16, 1811 was only a starter. It lasted two full days and the sky was filled with a thick dust and smoke and even several days later the sun shown through a brown dingy sky.

Many folks got down and prayed for forgiveness as they thought the "*end of times*" were upon them.

Indians all around knew that the Great Chief Tecumseh was not a liar and he was truly ruled by the Great Spirit. Many of the Indians that had ran away after the Tippecanoe battle now would began to come back to Tecumseh.

The British were thrilled with the new circumstances and that the Indians would truly be their ally. Now with their promise to the Indians that they would help drive the Americans back across the Blue Ridge Mountains, was what the Indians wanted to hear. The Indians would be ready to fight the Shemanese when the British picked up the musket and tomahawk.

Was Tecumseh still stomping his foot? On January 23, 1812 another 7.8 earthquake hit near New Madrid, Missouri and again an 8.2 quake hit on February 7, 1812. Each quake had loosened up the ground, rocks, and trees and the eastern half of what is now the United States was in a jumble. The last quake was the worst and did the most damage. Who could doubt Tecumseh now, after all he had given the prediction months before that the people would feel the earth shake when he stomped his foot.

Back in Tazewell County, Virginia the folks were thinking it must be close to the time that Jesus was coming back to claim His Church. Jesus had give warning as to the signs of His coming in Matthew Chapter 24: Verses 6-7.

> 6. *And you shall hear of wars and rumors of wars: see that ye be not troubled: for all these things must come to pass, but the end is not yet.*
> 7. *For nation shall rise against nation, and kingdom against kingdom: and there shall be famines, and pestilences, and earthquakes, in divers places.*

Hezekiah looked up this passage as it was so much on his mind. He read it to Rachel and some of the children that were around that evening.

"It sure looks like all of this is coming to pass," said Rachel.

"We are having wars and rumors all around the world and it looks like the British and the Indians are going to challenge us again," said Hezekiah.

"Yes it does and we sure have had the earthquakes and pestilences, and there are famines in some places," exclaimed Rachel.

"We have to be ready for the wars and for the coming of our Lord," replied Hezekiah. Then he had a long prayer of praise, thanksgiving, and of repentance.

All we can do is pray, follow the Lord Jesus Christ and be ready to fight our enemies when they come.

Back in the Indiana territory the Indians that had deserted the cause because of the shortcomings of Tenskwatawa were now reconsidering Tecumseh as their leader against the Shemanese. Some thought it prudent to start the fighting where the nearest whites lived. They began to burn cabins, kill white folks and plunder their goods up and down the Wabash plumb to the Mississippi. Once again the settlers were going out prepared by carrying their muskets wherever they went, even out to get wood, water or work in their fields. The attacks spread to the State of Ohio and even some in Kentucky.

William Hull, the Governor of the new Michigan Territory was sending out scouts and getting nothing but bad news. The Indians were building up in big numbers and they all carried the new British Muskets. Hull was in contact with the government in Washington and asking congress to give permission to attack the Indians and British at Fort Malden. He urged the capture of Canada before the forces became too great.

President Madison authorized Hull and gave him the rank of General. He would send regular troops and call up 1,200 Ohio Militia and equip them with supplies and new blue uniforms with red collars. He also would provide a cocked hat with a white plume for each man.

The headquarters were set up at Dayton, Ohio. Governor Meigs came to inspect the troops and meet with General Hull. They decided the best place to meet was in the McCullum's Tavern.

Now the new army of the northwest had 2,500 men and Hull accepted command from Governor Meigs. Hull had experience in soldiering as he served with General Anthony Wayne during the Revolution. Hull felt very positive as he looked at his well dressed and well supplied army. Hull was not the man he was forty years ago. Now he was fat and sluggish and not the best man to be the leader. They marched on the first day of June, 1812 and in about six days reached Urbana. More local men joined the army as they marched toward the north.

Word spread like wild fire that the United States had declared war on Great Britain. Every able bodied man was ready to serve if called. President James Madison had been urging

Congress for sometime to declare war. It was not just because of the Indians and British in the northwest, but the British had been boarding the American ships. The British had set up blockades to prevent goods to come from or go to France and other countries. It was hurting the United States badly.

General Hull took his army toward Detroit and the going got rough because there were no real roads to the north. It took the army over two weeks to breach the Maumee River, only 95 miles distant. The men were exhausted and many of the horses and mules died from exhaustion of pulling wagons through brush and knee deep swamps.

General Hull took control of the United States Ship Cuyahoga and had all the supplies loaded aboard her. He would send it ahead as he marched his army up the river. The General did the unthinkable thing of placing all of his papers and plans for the campaign on board. The Cuyahoga did not go too far before a British gunboat captured her and all of the supplies including Hull's plans. The information was forwarded to British General Isaac Brock.

Hull was unaware of this and his spies confirmed that Fort Malden was weak because reinforcements had not arrived. Hull commanded his army to move on Detroit, but when he got within about 15 miles he became plagued with the "what ifs". What if the attack cost many lives, what if the American General (Hull) was killed, what if Tecumseh unleashed his Indians on the settlers? Hull became so worried he turned his army back to Detroit, even though all the men were ready for a fight.

There was much talk about the earthquakes and the war with Great Britain. Who knew what this would bring after a time of peace and great growth of the United States. All of the citizens thought that we would beat them again and put the savages down for good.

Wars and Rumors of War

General Hull had not been informed that the Congress of the United States had declared war on Great Britain. General Hull settled in Detroit and then sent Major Thomas Van Horne with 600 men to escort the mail and meet a supply convoy under a Major William Brush located near the mouth of Raisin River.

Tecumseh and about 70 warriors along with the British Captain James Muir who had but 40 soldiers intercepted them with ambush and the first battle of the War of 1812. There were many battles and Tecumseh has one more Big Predictament

I need to reflect back to the battle of Thames as this is a turning point in the War of 1812. The Americans under General William Henry Harrison were pushing the British north. Tecumseh tried to shame the British General Proctor to take a stand and defeat the Americans. Proctor was satisfied to go deeper into Canada and take a stand there. Tecumseh and his warriors served as the rear guard as Proctor moved his army up the Thames Valley.

As you know Tecumseh was very mystical and had predicted many occurrences such as a solar eclipse, a comet, and an enormous earthquake besides many other small predictions.

He had one more prediction and it was to take place on October 5, 1813 at the battle of the Thames. He got up that morning and told his people that this is a good day to die and then gave them a prediction.

"Today I will be shot and will die, but I give my war club to my good friend Chaubenee, when he sees me fall, he is to rush to me and touch me with my war club, I will rise up and lead you to a great victory over the Shemanese!" said Tecumseh.

The Indians all sat quietly and listened to their great leader.

"If my most trusted friend, Chaubenee, cannot reach me and give me the touch, you will be defeated. If I and Chaubenee both die I want you to depart from the British and go home and learn to live with the Americans," explained the great Chief Tecumseh.

As the battle started in a rage, the 45 year old Tecumseh was felled with a lead ball from the Americans. Another Indian was seen running to Tecumseh, but a ball struck him and he dropped dead. The Indians saw this and they all dispersed into the shelter of the woodland and headed home.

Richard Mentor Johnson was given the credit of the shot that took Tecumseh down and this glory helped him be elected as vice-president to serve with President Martin Van Buren.

The Americans hated Tecumseh as a dreaded foe and they all wanted a piece of his hide, literally. Only old Simon Kenton was there to point out Tecumseh to the blood thirsty souvenir seekers. Simon had great respect for the Noble Indian Chief. Tecumseh as usual did not wear a lot of decorations and such when in battle as did some chiefs. He basically looked like a normal brave lying on the field of battle. Kenton saw Tecumseh, but pointed out a lesser chief as he knew the

Americans would butcher the great chief. It was awful how the Americans acted that day, the poor Indian they thought was Tecumseh was basically skinned; some took bigger parts such as ears and apiece of his scalp of long black hair. Some just took a feather or a piece of clothing. Tecumseh was spared of this disgrace because Simon Kenton did what he did.

Tecumseh is one of the most famous Native Americans in history. Some folks say it is his depiction on the Indian Head Penny. The name has been given to many Americans and all of the Indians had a hole in their heart for many years after Tecumseh died.

Who knows what may have happened if Tecumseh had rose again? Was the Great Spirit that led Tecumseh good or evil? One thing for sure, Tecumseh lived in a Spirit World.

Hezekiah's Spirit Lingers

Hezekiah and Rachel are my GGG Grandparents. Rachel was Native American and daughter of the Great Chief Cornstalk.

The winter of 1845 was especially hard for Hezekiah and Rachel Whitt. It seemed that one or the other was sick all winter.

James and Nancy Skaggs Whitt were a real blessing to them. Jonas was also over there almost every day to help in some way.

David Crockett Whitt was almost nine years old and doing the work of a man! Hannah was only six, and had become a big help in the kitchen. This was the way of good country families in 1845.

Jonas and James Whitt were helping the elderly Hezekiah and Rachel.

James Griffith, Crockett, and Hannah were helping their Paw, Jonas Whitt.

Winter would soon be over in Tazewell county 1846!

Hezekiah was so weak by the end of February that he hardly ever got out of bed.

Rachel was also sickly, but able to get up and stir around.

Jonas and James kept hoping with the spring their Paw would spring back to better health.

On Sunday the 28th of March 1846 at 8:06 A.M., God called the stately old Gentleman Hezekiah Whitt home. (Now the ghost story begins.)

What would the Whitt family do without their beloved grand leader? Everyone gathered at the Hezekiah House that day in disbelief! Rachel was so sad, even though she knew this day was coming. She tried to be brave in front of the entire family.

"You all know this is his birthday, don't you?" said Rachel.

"He lived a good life serving his family, his state and his country all the days of his life; bless his heart, he is eighty six today," stated Rachel.

"He turned over this morning and held me tight and kissed me goodbye," she said sobbing.

"Paw always said if I make it through March I always live another year!" I never knew what he meant, "He did not quiet make it through March this time," said James.

"I have heard him say that for years," replied Jonas.

"We have to get letters off to all the other children." Nancy interjected.

"They will not be able to get here for the funeral, but they will want to come home as soon as possible," James responded.

"Got to get word to town and to Elder David Young," James announced.

"I hate having to make plans like this," replied Jonas.

"I know what you mean," said James.

"Paw had lived a long good life, he is with Jesus now," Jones said.

"He would not come back here to all his aches and pains, even if he could," Jonas added.

"He loved his family dearly, but now he is in the love of Christ," said James.

James Griffith Whitt, Crockett Whitt, and Hannah Whitt (Children of Jonas and Susannah Whitt) were at Church this morning. They will be in shock when they get back and hear the sad news!

All the children and their families gathered that afternoon at the Hezekiah Whitt house. (In Baptist Valley, VA.) The house was full of Hezekiah's offspring. He was loved by all, except a few political foes! Even they respected him.
James Griffith saddled his horse and headed out to share the sad news. He was headed to find Elder David Young first and to let any one else he met know about the great loss of the Whitt family.

There would be a church service in the evening at most of the churches, so an announcement could be given then.

James Griffith made a long ride around Tazewell County that day. He carried the sad news far and wide. Everyone in Tazewell County knew or at least had heard of Hezekiah Whitt and would want to know about his demise.

James, Jonas,(Sons of Hezekiah) and all of the other local children of Hezekiah decided to have a meeting in the morning when things would be settled down. Funeral arrangements, had to be made, and many other things to consider. Letters would have to be written to all the kin that did not live near by. Even the will would have to go to probate, but that would not be mentioned for some time. Rachel was not well and her health had to be considered.

James and Jonas went to the barn to find the coffin. Hezekiah had it made several years before. Jonas had done most of the work on it and put it in storage in the barn loft under heavy canvas. The sons of Hezekiah climbed into the loft with tear filled eyes.

Jonas went right to it.

"It is right here," Jonas replied to James.

"This thing has been waiting here for about six or seven years, hope nothing has disturbed it," replied James.

They dragged it out into the open. They uncovered the fine coffin with care.

"It looks great", exclaimed Jonas.

The coffin was made of oak and trimmed out in walnut; it shined brightly under the rubbed in bee wax.

James commented, "Jonas I think this is some of your best work, it still looks brand new!"

"It was stored to last for years, I hoped I would never have to go and get it out," said Jonas.

"Paw wanted it ready, so no one would have to do hurry up job when he passed," said James.

"I remember him looking over his coffin," Jonas said.

"This is the nicest coffin I ever seen, it is fit for a King or President," Paw had related.

"We told him he was worthy of such a fine coffin, remember Jonas."

"Yes I do, he really liked it, I think he would come out and look at it from time to time, because I see it has been tampered with," replied Jonas.

"I heard him mention it every now and then, so he probably did," said James.

Jonas had his sons, John Bunyon and James Griffith, to help lower it down out of the loft. The four carried it to the house and set it up to lay their beloved Hezekiah in it.

Rachel and the women dressed Hezekiah in his finest suit, put on some rouge and good smelling perfume.

Jonas, James, and others lifted Hezekiah into his coffin.

Rachel broke down in loud lamentations.

James and Jonas held her tightly and the tears flowed like little rivers. The whole family fell into deep grieving! Wailing and weeping went on for some time.

The coffin was displayed in the sitting room so that the friends and family could visit with Hezekiah. The wake would be on the night of the March 29th. As was the custom many folks came to sit with the family, bringing plates of food and drinks. It seemed that the whole State of Virginia came by. So many people knew Hezekiah and wanted to pay their last respect.

Rachel was worn down and had to find seclusion in an upstairs bed room. Each one of the family grieved in a different way. Some tried to stay busy and not think on the matter, while others give into it and went to bed in depression. Yet others went through sessions of weeping.

David Crockett had a hard time accepting the fact that Grand paw Hezekiah would not be around to talk with him. Hannah was busy playing, trying to ignore the realization of what occurred. Jonas sat down and talked to both of them, explaining that Grand paw went to Heaven to live with Jesus!

Crockett understood somewhat, but Hannah kept saying, "He is in there in the coffin."

Jonas tried to explain that when people die their body stays here but their spirit leaves and goes to Heaven or Hell. Don't worry about Grand paw going to Hell. He was a devoted Christian so he is in Heaven with Jesus.

Jonas explained, "Grand paw is up there walking around Heaven with no pain, and is real happy, he can run and jump like you do!"

"He is waiting for Grand maw and the rest of us to join him some day, so we have to prepare ourselves to go there by living a Christian life," Jonas added.

The morning of March 30th came and Jonas got some pine tar. He spread some all around the edge of the lid on the coffin. The coffin was sealed and secured, not to be opened again.

A big breakfast was cooked that morning for all that was there and the procession would start at 11:00 A.M. There was some scripture reading and remembrances by the different friends and family.

At about 10:45 A.M., Jonas told Crockett to get Hezekiah's flag and go out in the yard to start the line.

Six strong men were chosen to carry Hezekiah to the top of the hill where he would be laid to rest. James and Jonas took Rachel out to follow behind the coffin. Next followed every family member, then the friends of Hezekiah would join the sad procession.

Jonas motioned to David Crockett to start the trek to the grave site. Jonas had already given him instruction to walk slowly and hold the flag high and proud.

Crockett took the first step and the men carrying Hezekiah followed suit.

On top of the little hill a grave had been dug and benches erected for the family. Elder David Young and a choir from the church were waiting.

Almost seven years has past since another sad line of people climbed this little hill.

Jonas and his children could not help but think of that day they laid Susannah to rest.

David Crockett Whitt led the procession with honor! He held the old flag high for his Grand paw. He walked slowly allowing everyone to keep up. Hezekiah would be so proud of his grandson, as he looked down on this celebration of his life. Rachel did not tire as Jonas and James helped her along.

Many people were waiting at the Green Mountain road to join in the march. The whole hill was covered when everyone closed in to hear the minister preach the funeral.

The lay of the land for the trip from the house to the grave yard was down a slight hill, cross the Green Mountain Road and up the top of the Cemetery Hill. The distance was a little more than an eighth of a mile.

Elder David Young stepped up to address the family and friends of Hezekiah Whitt.

Crockett had taken the flag off the pole and draped it over the beautiful coffin and taken a seat beside of Jonas and the family.

The Elder spoke loud so that every ear could hear. He opened with the Lords Prayer read scripture from Revelation and sat down. The choir stood and sang a couple of hymns. Once again the Elder David Young stood; he was going to give the Eulogy of Hezekiah Whitt.

Gentleman Justice of the Peace Hezekiah Whitt has been a model for us all to follow. At the young age of seventeen, he along with his father Reverend Richard Whitt took the Patriot's Oath on September 13th 1777. Hezekiah saw action several times in the defense of Virginia and this United States. He laid his life on the line time after time so that we could enjoy the freedoms this country stands for.

After the war was won, Hezekiah was appointed along with eight other gentlemen by Governor Patrick Henry to serve as Gentleman Justices of the Peace to establish this great county of Tazewell.

Hezekiah was chosen because he was trustworthy, loyal, and brave. Hezekiah has been a servant to the people of the United States, The State of Virginia, and the County of Tazewell most of his life.

He was also a servant of the Lord Jesus Christ.

He has been a faithful husband and father to his family.

Hezekiah will be missed by his loving wife Rachel, by his seven children, all of his grandchildren and great grandchildren. I dare say

Hezekiah will be missed many years into the future by the offspring of his seed, if the world still stands.

He is lifted high and respected by all who know him. He will be missed by his associates and neighbors.

Today we lay to rest the body of a great man. We as believers in Christ know that Hezekiah is in the presence of Jesus Christ. Hezekiah wishes that we cry no more, but rejoice for him. He has fought the good fight, he has run the good race, and now he has found rest with the Lord.

After the Elder had finished the service, the old Betsy Ross type flag was folded and given to Rachel. Hezekiah had this flag since early in the war, almost seventy years.

After the Funeral most of the people shook hands with the family and started making their way toward their respective homes. It looked like the whole County of Tazewell was at the gathering to honor the late Hezekiah and his family.

It began to rain. The ladies began to bring out their umbrellas.

Jonas quoted the old saying; *"Happy the dead the rain falls upon, happy the bride the sunshine's upon."*

The next few days things did not get back to normal, how could they? Hezekiah Whitt was dead and Rachel was not adjusting! She was over on the other side of the mental river.

She kept talking like Hezekiah was still living in the house with her. She said that he was still there; she had seen him all around the house. Rachel was not afraid of her life long friend, lover, and companion. She would go about her day, talking to the deceased Hezekiah.

James and Nancy almost believed that Hezekiah was there also. Jonas was over to see his Maw everyday, but did not believe what seemed to be true. Could it be that Hezekiah was waiting around for something before he moved on to the realm of glory?

Elder Young was sent for. When he arrived James and Nancy had a talk with him before he went in to see Rachel. He said that he had heard of things like this, but never dealt with it personally. He read a few passages in his Bible and prayed before he went in to visit Rachel.

Elder Young went in alone to visit with Rachel.

"Good morning Elder," she spoke in greeting!

"Good morning to you Rachel, I thought I would stop by and see you this morning on my rounds."

"Well come on in I will get you a nice cup of tea and something sweet, I have some apple cobbler, and some cookies, "Rachel said.

"Which would you like?" she asked while getting the tea.

"A cookie would be nice," he answered.

As she sat down with him at the kitchen table, he asked how she was doing since the funeral.

"Well just fine I reckon, Hezekiah is still here with Me." she answered.

The hair on the back of the Elder's neck stood up. He thought she would try to hide the fact that she was seeing things.

"What do you mean Rachel?" Elder Young asked.

"You saw him in that beautiful coffin." added the Elder.

"You followed him all the way to the cemetery; you know he is buried over on cemetery hill, don't you?" asked Elder Young.

"Well Elder, I ain't crazy, I seen all of that, but my dear Hezekiah come back home with me," exclaimed Rachel.

"He is sitting over there in that chair, I can see him smiling at me right now," Rachel stated.

Goose bumps rose up all over the Elder.

"Rachel, I cannot see Hezekiah, you know he is gone on to be with the Lord." said the Elder.

"Well not yet he ain't, he told me he was waiting for me!" replied Rachel.

"What do you mean Rachel, waiting for you?" asked Elder Young.

"Well waiting! You know! I will be going with him real soon!" said Rachel.

Elder David Young was in shock, he had never seen anything like it. Rachel was completely calm, and normal it seemed! Yet Rachel talked to Hezekiah right in front of the Elder.

"Rachel, does Hezekiah answer you?" said Elder Young.

"Sure he does, I can't understand why no one else sees him" replied Rachel.

He is so happy, and has no pain.

"He told me I would be going with him soon, he told me it is wonderful, no pain, no tears, and he is young again," said Rachel in a most serious tone.

"How does he look to you Rachel, you say young?" asked the Elder.

"He appears to be young like he was when I fell in love with him," she replied.

"Hezekiah thinks it is funny that you are asking me all these questions." she added.

"I think He wants to be alone with me," she added.

"Please elder, do you mind to leave us alone, and go about your work?" Rachel asked.

"Yes Ma-am, I do have things I need to do, if you want to talk again, just let me know," said Elder Young.

"I will." replied Rachel!

Rachel said, "Elder you be ready to have my funeral, It wouldn't be to far off," and she smiled!

"Now Rachel, you don't know that," Elder Young replied.

"You can count on it," Hezekiah doesn't know what day, but said "I would be coming with him to see Jesus real soon!"

The Elder was a bit shaken inside, but tried not to show it.

"Well Rachel, if I am still around, I will give you a good funeral," Elder Young assured her.

"I will be back to see you in a few days," he said.

The Elder went out to the yard to speak with James, Nancy, and Jonas.

"Well Elder, what did you find out?" asked James.

"I hate to admit it, but I think the spirit of Hezekiah is with your mother," he said.

"She seems just fine and is quiet convincing about seeing Hezekiah, I sense no evil in the house, she told me to be ready to have her funeral real soon," stated the Elder.

"Brother have you gone around the bin," Jonas asked the Elder?

"No Jonas, I am telling you what I think after being in there with Rachel, sometimes Indian folk know things" the Elder replied.

"If I were you I would prepare for, well what she says," he added.

"She said that she would be going with Hezekiah soon, have you sent letters out to the other children yet?" asked Elder Young.

"No, we put that off until things settled down some," said James.

"I would do it today, the other children may be able to see Rachel before she goes on." he answered.

Jonas was a little angry inside, because the Elder was talking like this. Elder Young sensed this and explained to Jonas.

"I am sorry Jonas, I am only telling you what I believe, there is no evil in it," said the Elder.

"Rachel wants to go to her beloved husband, she wants to go and meet the Lord Jesus," Elder Young said.

Jonas nodded, "Thanks Elder Young, I know you mean no harm."

"What do you suggest we do, when Maw is talking to paw?" James asked.

"Go along with her, it will be pleasing to her and maybe Hezekiah too," the Elder said.

With that the Elder prayed for the family, mounted his horse, and headed across Green Mountain.

Young David Crockett Whitt has been about, listening to all the talk about Rachel. He thought to himself, I bet Grand paw Hezekiah is here waiting for Grand maw Rachel. I know if Grand paw is still here, he wouldn't hurt any body. I hope he will let me see him, like he does Grand maw. Young Crockett was like everyone else, he could not understand what was going on with Grand maw Rachel. Why did Grand paw have to die? Why does Grand maw want to die? Some things are not meant for us to understand was his conclusion. David Crockett never saw the spirit of Hezekiah, even though he believed Grand maw Rachel did.

Letters to Hezekiah's other children. Richard Nelson, John Bunyon, Rebecca, and Susannah were written and mailed out. The other children were already contacted.

Richard (Devil Dick) Nelson Whitt lived in Carter County Kentucky. John Bunyon lived in Floyd County Kentucky. Rebecca and Susannah lived in the far west side of Tazewell County. (Present McDowell County, West Virginia).

Griffy Whitt lived clean across the waters of the Mississippi River in Missouri.

Crockett is anxious to meet his Uncles from that famous place called Kentucky. He hoped to hear stories of Daniel Boone and Simon Kenton. He wanted to hear about the Indian Wars that took place there only a few years past.

Grand maw Rachel never changed, as far as the relationship she had with the spirit of Hezekiah. Each day Rachel seemed to get weaker and spent her days in bed or in the sitting room. Crockett spent much time visiting with Grand maw Rachel. She told him many stories of the old days and continued to speak to the invisible Hezekiah.

James, Nancy, and Jonas were all worried about her. Her mind seemed sharp and crisp except for the continued talking to the deceased Hezekiah. The Elder David Young came by every day or two to pray with the family and visit Rachel. Any word from the sons in Kentucky he would ask?

"No not yet, we pray they will get to see Maw before she passes," answered James.

"Maw gets weaker each day it seems," said Jonas.

Elder Young had an idea, what if you put Rachel in the buggy and take her to visit Hezekiah's grave? Reckon that might turn her back around? Jonas looked at James, James looked at Nancy. It is worth a try, we will do it. James went in and talked to Rachel.

"Maw let's get you ready and take a buggy ride," said James.

"Why son," she asked?

"I am doing just fine here with your paw," Rachel added.

It made James and the other children so sad to see her this way.

"Maw please, do this for me," James said.

"Well I reckon I can, where are we going," she asked?

"I want to take you over to the cemetery so you can visit paws grave," James said.

"If it is that important to you I will go," she said.

"It makes no sense to me, when Hezekiah is right here," she added.

The family got Rachel up and dressed. They carried her out to the buggy. All the children went with her except those from Kentucky as they had not got home yet. They talked about the nice coffin, the great crowd that attended the funeral, and the good sermon the Elder preached that day. Rachel went along with everything the children were trying to do.

"I remember all of this, children," Rachel confirmed.

"Your paw really enjoyed all that you done for him. He was impressed with the crowd that day," she said.

The children all looked at each other in disbelief!

Well, Jonas was thinking, nothing ventured, nothing gained! I am beginning to believe paw is still here with maw.

They took her home and put her back to bed because she told them, "I am bone tired children."

It was about the end of May 1846, and finally two riders rode up to the Hezekiah Whitt House.

James spoke up, "Glory be, look, there is John and Richard."

Crockett was there so James sent him over to get Jonas and the rest of the family. After Crockett shook hands with these two famous uncles he headed home to fetch Jonas.

John and Richard were famous to Crockett because of all the stories he had heard about them. John and Richard were both big strong men. They both looked like Hezekiah, except they were both much more massive. They were tall like Hezekiah and well filled out with muscle.

Crockett thought to himself, I am glad I don't have to fight these big men. I am glad they are my uncles.

"Paw, Paw," Crockett hollered as he ran in the door.

"What is it son?"

"Uncle John and Richard are over to Grand maws," said the excited Crockett.

James Griffith, son of Jonas was in the house at the time.

"Let's get over there, I barely remember them," said James.

"Take your horse James Griffith, after you meet them, would you mind to make a ride and inform the rest of the family?" Jonas asked.

"I will be glad to, I do want to see them first," replied James Griffith.

James and Nancy explained the situation to Richard and John Bunyon, before they went in to see their maw.

Richard looked at James, "you mean maw thinks paw is still alive?"

"No!" James answered, *"She sees his spirit and says he is waiting for her!"*

Richard looks at John in disbelief.

"Can you understand this brother," asked Richard.

"No" answered John!

"Let's go see what they are talking about," John added.

Richard and John went in to see Mother Rachel.

She looked at them and said, "There is my babies from Kane tuck."

"You are a sight for sore eyes," she said as she rose up to hug them.

She looked over at an empty chair, "look Hezekiah, John Bunyon and Richard are here from Kentucky."

They both looked at the empty chair and back at each other.

Rachel saw their disbelief, "Oh don't worry boys, for some reason I am the only one that can see your paw."

Rachel asked, "Have you heard from your brother Griffy?"

No maw," we wondered if he had got the word about paw passing."

"I am so sorry maw that we didn't get home in time to see paw," said Richard.

"Don't fret son, your paw understands, he is smiling at you right now," said Rachel.

Richard just didn't know what to say.

John changes the subject, "Maw, you look good, how have you been?"

"Well, I am bone tired boys," Rachel responded.

"I will be a leaving you before long." she added.

"Now maw you don't know that;" exclaimed Richard.

"Well honey I can't live forever," she said, and let it go at that.

John Bunyon Whitt and Richard (Devil Dick) Whitt had a lot of catching up to do. They had many stories to tell and many to hear. They both came by horseback, leaving the wives and families back in Kentucky because of the time. They did not want to miss seeing Rachel, before it was too late. She seemed to be very mentally alert, except for the Hezekiah thing. Richard and John had not ruled out that their paw Hezekiah was visiting in the spirit.

Brother Griffy and his wife Patty from Missouri, show up the very next day. They came in a hurry on horseback also. They got in to Tazewell County about an hour before dark.

John and Richard are sitting around talking about Kentucky and their trips coming home. Jonas and David Crockett seem really interested. The family has been visiting all day. Rachel is tired, but has sat up most of the day. She still looks to an empty chair and speaks to the invisible Hezekiah. The sound of riders is heard out back. James gets up and heads to the back door. I wonder who that could be this time of day, he said.

He opens the door and there is Griffith Whitt and his wife Patty. "Its brother Griffy," James exclaimed. Everyone arose to greet their brother from way out in Missouri.

Rachel heard all the commotion, "Did I hear you say Griffiy?" she said." Yes Maw, that's right, Griffy and Patty just rode up," said Nancy. Griffiy and Patty tied up their horses and were in the house in an instant.

Jonas was thinking, we didn't get to tell them about Maw seeing Paw all the time.

Griffy and Patty hugged their way through the crowd on the way to see Rachel. As Griffy came into the bedroom, Rachel praised the Lord for seeing her son from so far away.

"Yes maw, It is me and Patty, we have come as fast as we could to see you," said Griffy.

Rachel turns to the empty chair, and says, "look Hezekiah, Griffy and Patty are here."

Griffy looks in the direction of the empty chair and back to his maw.

Rachel sees the confusion on Griffy's face and speaks up," Don't worry son, I know it may seem strange to you but Hezekiah is here waiting for me!"

Griffy is dumbfounded!

"Maw I thought paw was buried at the end of March," said Griffy.

"Well son, his body is over on the hill, but your paw come back home with me," answered Rachel.

"Nothing to be alarmed about, he is such a handsome man, looks like he did when we got married," she continued.

Griffy thinks it is time to change the subject, "How are you doing maw?" he asked.

"Not too good honey, I am getting weaker each day it seems," she said.

"I thought I would be gone with your paw to meet Jesus by now," she said.

"Well, we never know when we will get the call," said Griffy, "You might out live all of us"

"No son, Hezekiah would not be here waiting if that was so," she answered.

"I wish you all could see him, he is so pleased to see all of you here with me," said Rachel.

Nancy opens up with another line of talk, "bet you all are starved to death," she said.

Griffy and Patty answered, "We could eat, we have not eaten a good meal since we left home."

"Well we have a pan of fried up fish, and I can get you some good grub to go with it in a couple of shakes," Nancy said.

"If you don't want the fish we can slice you off some good old Virginia ham," she added.

"Now don't go to no trouble, anything will be good," Patty answered.

Griffy turns back to Mother Rachel.

"Maw and paw, we are going to take care of our horses and get some vittles," he said.

"Then we will spend some time with you, If you need to sleep, we will be here tomorrow to catch up on all the news," Griffy added.

Rachel smiles, she is glad that Griffy acknowledged that his paw was present.

"Alright Griffy, take care of the horses, eat and get some rest; we will visit all day tomorrow," said Rachel.

Griffy and Patty both go over and give Rachel a kiss.

Griffy and Jonas go out to take care of their mounts.

"What is going on with maw?" he asks Jonas.

"We are not sure, she is sharp as a tack, except that she insists that paw is waiting for her, sorry we didn't get to warn you before you walked into that, you handled it real well brother," said Jonas.

Griffy looks at the young straight boy with Jonas.

"Now who is this young man?" Griffy asked.

"Griffy this is my youngest son David Crockett Whitt," replied Jonas.

Griffy stuck out his hand to Crockett. Crockett clasped the big hand of Uncle Griffy Whitt.

"Glad to meet you sir," said Crockett.

"Glad to meet you, you know you have a famous name don't you son?" asked Griffy.

"Yes sir, a lot to live up to I guess," said Crockett.

Griffy laughed.

Jonas helped Griffy unload the horses, and instructed Crockett to take them to the barn.

"Now son water Uncle Griffy's horses and give them a good feeding of corn and oats," Jonas instructed.

"Yes sir," was the answer as Crockett led the tired horses to the barn. He did all that Jonas had said and also dried the horses down and ran a curry comb over them.

Crockett was thinking, the horses of Uncle John, Richard, and Griffy are of the best stock. I think they must be thoroughbreds. Kentucky is famous for their horses. Jake was one of the few that compared.

Crockett was also thinking that Griffy looked like Richard and John, but was much leaner. He is more like Grand paw Hezekiah and Paw.

The Whitt's talked about an hour past dark. In June that is late for farming people.

Jonas was the first to say, "We better get going so you can get in bed, tomorrow is another day and we can visit most of it.

"Maw will be fresh in the morning I hope, so she can visit all she wants," said Griffy.

Jonas and Crockett headed back to Indian Creek Farm, after he offered a bed to any who might want to go with him.

Nancy spoke up, "thanks Jonas, we will be able to bed everyone down here."

"See you all on the morrow, and goodnight all," Jonas said as they disappeared into the night.

Next day the 2nd day of June, the Whitt's had a full blown reunion. By now every Whitt in the Valley had heard the news of Griffy, John, and Richard coming in to visit. The women got together and cooked up a great feast for the family to eat. Rachel was quite pert at least for the first half of the day. Each brother took turns telling story after story. Crockett listened intently, wishing that all of these stories were written down in a book.

After all the brothers talked, the children of Jonas told of some happenings in their own lives. The trip from Montgomery County and the bandit episode was told by James Griffith (son of Jonas). John Bunyon (son of Jonas) told the story of killing the bear on the first weekend in Tazewell County.

Even Crockett spoke up, he told of the great shooting match, and his big brother James Griffith beat every one in Tazewell County.

Stories of rolling hills, the Ohio River, and the Mississippi river were told. Even stories that were told to them about Kentucky's early days were rekindled. Stories of Blue Jacket, Little Turtle, and Tecumseh, and the Indian escapades were retold with exaggeration! Names like Daniel Boone, Simon Kenton, and John Logan were also mentioned.

Kentucky was once the great hunting ground of many Indian nations. This great state was worth fighting for. It is now a tame peaceful land with rich soil and great grazing for cattle and horses. At one time the rolling bluegrass lands teemed with Elk, buffalo and wolf packs that followed them.

Young David Crockett Whitt asked about his namesake, "What about old Davy Crockett?"

"Was he a big name in Kentucky?" asked Crockett.

"Not really" Uncle Richard answered, "he was in Tennessee mostly and moved on to Texas."

"He did about the same in Tennessee as Boone did in Kentucky," Richard said.

"I don't know if they ever met or not, Boone would be older than Crockett" he surmised. Uncle Griffy spoke up, "I know that Daniel Boone moved to Missouri after he got closed in on in Kentucky."

"Boone had said, "When he saw the smoke of his neighbor's chimney, I don't have enough elbow room.""

"He is buried in Missouri not too far from where we live," Griffy added.

Also mention of the great earthquake of 1811 was told. It was said that the great Chief Tecumseh predicted it. Tecumseh said, "when I stomp my foot it will be felt for hundreds of miles." "That would be the sign for all Indians to come together and run the pale faces back across the mountains," said Griffy.

Everyone had a chance to tell stories.

Jonas said, "I wish paw was here to add to the stories."

"He had a bunch of them, and he was not bad to exaggerate," said Richard.

"Yes," answered James, "Paw was not one to brag, I feel his presence here anyway!"

After a week of visiting with Rachel and the entire family, the three brothers decided they better start back home. Richard had brought a letter with him from Doctor Samuel Truitt, of Greenup County Kentucky. It was sent to Jonas because Richard had told him about the skills he had. Jonas was an expert millwright and house builder. Doctor Truitt wanted to build two grist mills up in Greenup County, Kentucky.

"I thought you lived in Carter County," Jonas said.

"I do, but Greenup County is the next county over, it borders on the Ohio River. I met Doctor Truitt by chance when I made a trip up that way," said Richard.

He talked about the need for a gristmill and one thing led to another.

I told him, I would bring you a letter and see what you think about it.

"Well for now, I will say no, I ain't about to move off long as maw is sick," Jonas said.

"Some day in the future I may entertain that idea, you can tell Truitt that I am considering the idea," Jonas continued.

The three brothers decided to travel together on their journey back to Kentucky. You can't be too careful, bad people are still watching for an easy target. They were to travel the Kentucky Turnpike to Floyd County. Then Richard and Griffy would follow the Big Sandy a way further before heading into Carter County. Then of course Griffy and Patty would ride west and cross the Mississippi in western Kentucky.

The three sons were reluctant to leave Rachel, but they had to get back to families and farms. Rachel understood she kissed each one on that cool morning in June before they started back.

Crockett hated to see his uncles depart as well as the whole Whitt family did.

Crockett and Jonas both had a hankering to see Kentucky some day.

Rachel seems about the same, she still speaks to Hezekiah as if he never died. She missed her children after they left.

The 20th of June 1846 Rachel did not eat a thing. She was so weak she could hardly turn over.

As evening came to Hezekiah Whitt House, Rachel summoned her family around her. She spoke in whispers, and eye gestures, portraying her love for each family member. She said that she could see a beautiful river and Hezekiah and Jesus were waiting for her. There were so many beautiful trees and flowers. Angels were abounding!

"Children, I am going home!" she said in a whisper.

Rachel slipped off into a coma. Her body was shutting down and her legs and arms were as cold as winter.

Nancy asks us to gather around and sing some hymns.

"Rachel will be able to hear us," she said.

James got a song book and lined each verse aloud and then the whole family sang the song verse by verse. This went on for about an hour and then Rachel smiled and gave up the ghost. Jonas went to the clock and stopped it at 11:11 PM.

The family made tentative plans. Different ones would sit up with their beloved mother through the night. Word would go out early in the morning so that final plans could be made. Jonas and James would take the first three hours of watch. Later others would be awakened to come and sit with the beloved Rachel. First light the ladies would come and bath Rachel and put her in a favorite dress. A coffin was already prepared, because of recent events. Jonas and James had worked on the coffin with love.

As Jonas and James sat and talked in the bedroom. They had reflected on all that had gone on since their Paw died. They begin to talk about Rachel seeing Hezekiah, and seeing the realms of glory.

Grave of Hezekiah Whitt. 1761 to 1846

"I think it is because of the Indian blood that flowed through her veins," James said.

"That would explain a lot, I have always heard that Indians have an inside line to the spirit world." Jonas said.

"Me too," replied James.

"Bless her heart, she and paw can go on to glory now," exclaimed Jonas.

Rachel was Native American and the daughter of the Great Chief Cornstalk. Was she able to see the *"Spirit"* of her beloved Hezekiah?

This is a likeness of Chief Cornstalk.

He is my G G G G Grandfather. He was murdered at Fort Randolph, Point Pleasant, WV.

Murders at the Point

Source: The Book, "The Patriot, Hezekiah Whitt"

Chief Cornstalk, the principal Chief of the Shawnee, has toiled within himself as to what course to take. Hamilton, the red coat British leader working out of Detroit, was doing a good job of inciting all the Indian factions from New York to Illinois. The Shawnee and Delaware has held back, but with the Wyandot, Mingo, Miami, Ottawa, and Illinois already taking up the hatchet, plus the Cherokee and Creeks from the south, what choice is left for Cornstalk.

Chief Cornstalk talked to every person that he respected great and small, male and female, to gain advice. Cornstalk was in a lose, lose, situation. If he stayed neutral he may even have to fight the British and his red brothers of the other tribes. The British brought many gifts even into the Shawnee towns. The other tribes belittled some of the Shawnee braves, because they were not for another war. Some even called the great Chief Cornstalk a little squaw.

Chief Cornstalk was as brave as any person walking upon the earth. He was also as wise as any person, yet he was caught in a trap between the many factions of the time.

At last he decided to fight with his red brothers if it came to that, but being an honorable man he must go to Fort Randolph at Point Pleasant. He would go to the very spot where the battle was fought three years earlier. The Shemanese (whites) had built a fort on the Virginia (Now West Virginia) side of the Ohio River to keep the Indians on their side of the river. Only thing the Shemanese had crossed over to the Indian side many times and shot at every Indian they saw.

Cornstalk would go and talk to the white chief Captain Arbuckle in the fort. He would explain his stance and give warning that war was coming. Cornstalk was honorable and if he talked to the Captain, surely he would be honorable also. Since the treaty had been broken many times during the past three years in smaller ways, and war was imminent, Cornstalk would give warning to the Shemanese man to man.

Chief Cornstalk conversed with his friend Red Hawk the Chief of a smaller tribe called the Delaware. Red Hawk was a good ally and friend and had respected the decision of the great Chief Cornstalk. Cornstalk asks Red Hawk to travel with him to the fort of the Shemanese. He did not want to take a large force with him to alarm the Shemanese and maybe start an unplanned war.

So on Tuesday, October 7, 1777, Chief Cornstalk, Chief Red Hawk and an unnamed trusted

Shawnee brave crossed the waters of the great Ohio River from what is now Gallipolis, Ohio.

They paddled the single bark-canoe through the cool flat waters on that October day, to the ugly walled wooden fort that marked the spot where so much blood was poured out three years earlier.

The hills were beautiful with the colors of fall. The hues of red, yellow, brown and green painted a picture that no man could duplicate. We can only imagine what thoughts were going through the Chief's head. Was it on the beauty of the day, the past battle and the many slain tribesmen, or more on choosing words to tell the Shemanese Chief, Captain Arbuckle?

Within minutes of the canoe sliding its nose on the Virginia shore, loud voices could be heard.

"Injuns, Injuns, coming up the bank of the Ohio," shouted guards at their posts on the Palisade wall.

"How many?" screamed another voice from deep inside the fort?

"Three, I only see three," shouted the sentry on the wall.

In a minute more a detail of ten armed men ran to meet the two chiefs and the brave. Cornstalk stood straight and brave to greet the whites. He held up his arm as a sign of peace.

"Cornstalk come, talk to white Chief!" Cornstalk said in a grunting broken English dialect.

The armed detail kept their muskets at ready as one of them spoke,   "Come on Injuns, I will take you to the Captain."

Chief Cornstalk frowned at the Shemanese and walked stately toward the open gate with Red Hawk and the brave close on his heels.

Chief Cornstalk turned to Red Hawk and spoke lowly in Shawnee, "the Shemanese fear even three brave Indians!"

Red Hawk nodded and smiled in agreement.

Captain Arbuckle stepped out of a large room within the log structure. He put his arm up in a sign of peace to the approaching Indians. As they got close Captain Arbuckle spoke up sarcastically, "What can I do for you gentlemen today?"

Chief Cornstalk answered, "Come talk, White Chief!"

Captain Arbuckle commanded the armed guard to show the Indians into his office and put down their muskets. As the muskets were lowered Chief Cornstalk nodded to Captain Arbuckle in approval.

Captain Arbuckle led the Indians to his office which was a spacious log structure back against the outer wall. Next Captain Arbuckle sat down behind his crude desk. The two chiefs approached with the brave behind them. They stood in front of the desk and were not asked to have a seat.

"I am Cornstalk," said the chief.

"This Red Hawk," he continued.

"Why did you come here?" Asked Captain Arbuckle?

"Honor, I come talk honor, hard time coming," answered the Chief.

"What do you mean, hard times are coming?" ask Captain Arbuckle.

"Three years go by since talk at Camp Charlotte, I gave word to keep peace, stay on our side of Ohio, and not fight Shemanese," stated the great Chief.

"Much water flow since and we have talk treaty, never sign paper, but try to keep treaty, since this you Shemanese have war between you," exclaimed Chief Cornstalk.

"Yes Chief, the Red Coats have bared down on us Americans, we must throw them off so we can be our own nation," explained Captain Arbuckle.

"I come today, Shemanese break treaty too many times; we can not hold back, young braves talk to Red Coats, get much gifts. I no longer want hold them back! We have suffered much from

Shemanese, and there is no more treaty, I come to you in honor to tell this you!" stated the great Chief.

Captain Arbuckle rose up and ordered the soldiers to take the three Indians into custody.

"We are at war with the Shawnee again, you three will be my hostages against attack," stated Captain Arbuckle.

The three Indians were surprised but did not try to fight back. Chief Cornstalk thought if he came in honor he would be treated in honor. The Indians looked at each other in amazement and followed the soldiers to a holding cell just on the other side of the office wall. This was a guardhouse for law breakers of the army. The guards released a soldier from the cell and shoved the Indians into the room.

"Shemanese have no honor!" stated Red Hawk.

Chief Cornstalk grunted in agreement.

Captain Arbuckle figured that if he had the big chief, the Indians would not attack Fort Randolph. He ordered that the Indians be treated good and well fed while they were prisoners.

Next day another canoe is paddled across the great Ohio by a single Indian. Since Cornstalk and the others did not return across the river, Elinipsico, the son of Cornstalk came to see about his father.

Elinipsico went through the same drill as the other Indians had the day before. He stood in front of Captain Arbuckle's desk and asks about his father.

"I come to find my father, since he did not return across the Ohio, I saw his canoe on the bank, where is Chief Cornstalk and Red Hawk?" ask Elinipsico.

"Oh! They are just fine, they are visiting us for a few days," stated Captain Arbuckle.

The guards displayed an evil grin at his words.

"Will you take me to my father?" asked Elinipsico

"Sure will, you boys take this fellow back to visit his daddy," stated the Captain.

The soldiers escorted Elinipsico to the guardhouse, opened the door and shoved him in.

"My son, why did you come here?" asked Chief Cornstalk.

"You didn't come back across the Great River, so I came to see about you," answered Elinipsico.

"You should not have come, these dogs have no honor and are holding us hostage!" exclaimed Red Hawk.

"Who can figure out a white man, they make no sense and lie so easily," stated Elinipsico.

"Why do they hold us?" asked Elinipsico without taking a breath.

"Sit down here on this floor and we will reason together," said Chief Cornstalk as he lowered his hand toward the puncheon floor.

As they sat down Elinipsico noticed that the room was very dark. The only light came in from the back wall where two gun ports were located, and they had only one candle burning.

"Do they think we are badgers or groundhogs?" asked Elinipsico.

Cornstalk took out his pipe and filled it with kinnikinnick, took the candle that was handed to him, and lit the aromatic blend. The others waited patiently for their chief to finish.

"Well son we are not ground animals, these white dogs think that our warriors will not attack if they hold us, we must be patient and see what the Great Spirit has in store for us," Chief Cornstalk calmly said.

"Do you know what day this is?" asked Chief Red Hawk.

"Yes brother, I know this day has meaning, three years ago we and the Shemanese struggled here. I think back, if we did this, or if I did that could we have defeated the Shemanese? Would we even be sitting here in the darkness wondering if we will see the sun again, if not for that thing or this thing? The Great Spirit has blessed his red children and now he may take us to his bosom before we leave here," explained the Great Chief.

The chief passed around the pipe and each took it and inhaled the soothing smoke. After a few minutes of silence the unnamed, but trusted brave that accompanied the Chiefs spoke up.

"Matchemenetoo, Matchementetoo, (evil spirit, the devil) Shemanese (White Soldiers.) is full of Matchemenetoo!" stated the brave.

Chief Cornstalk reached over and touched the brave on his knee as he was sitting cross-legged in front of him.

"Be brave, all of you, if the Great Spirit calls us we shall go bravely, are we not Indians?" asked the Great Chief.

The other three nodded their heads in the dim light. Smoked the pipe and took turns telling stories of the good old days, before the Shemanese damaged Mother Earth. Cornstalk told about the days when food was plentiful.

"We hardly done any work at all, we spent much time making new little Indians," laughed Chief Cornstalk.

The other three Indians laughed out loud. The guards outside the door wondered what on earth the Indians could be laughing about in their circumstances.

Chief Cornstalk was doing this to take his brothers minds off their plight. He knew deep down that they may never ride freely on in the grasslands, enjoy a sunset, or even see the sun again.

The cracks of gun shots could be heard across the Kanawha River. The four Indians became silent as they listened intently.

A soldier from the fort just paddled across the Kanawha River and came running to the fort. The gate was opened to receive him. He was one of two men that had gone out early to do some deer hunting. He and his companion were ambushed about a mile from the fort.

"Them Red Devils jumped us just down the river bout a mile, they fired at us and we turned to find cover, John was hit bad, so I took off to get away. After I was a piece off I stopped and looked back. They were hacking on poor John. I took a real good aim and let loose on the one that looked like a chief. The shot knocked him plumb off the ground. They looked at me and here they come. I high-tailed it to the canoe and paddled fast as I could," stated the soldier.

Captain Arbuckle stepped up and ordered a patrol of a dozen soldiers to go out and bring John back and destroy the enemy if possible.

After about two hours passed the men could be heard returning to the fort. They had John's body what was left of it. The whole fort was in an uproar. A mob was formed by the returning soldiers and the other men joined in.

"Revenge, Revenge," yelled the men as they broke into the part of the fort where the guard house was located.

"Stand and be brave brothers, today we will be with the Great Spirit," exclaimed Chief Cornstalk.

"My son you were sent here to die with your father, rise up and stand bravely," continued Cornstalk.

All four of the Indians rose up and stood bravely as the noise came toward the door. The guards that were outside the door stepped aside as the mob appeared. The door was thrown open and the mob was taken aback for an instant as they witnessed the bravery of the four Shawnee Indians.

Finally the leader of the mob broke the silence by saying, *"By Gawd, it is that devil Cornstalk!"*

He fired his musket and all the others followed suit and all four defenseless brave Indians slumped to the floor. Chief Cornstalk had no less than eight lead balls pass through his body. It was simply murder. An honorable man and his tribesmen were killed trying to do an honorable thing and give warning to the whites at Fort Randolph.

As Chief Cornstalk lay with his life's blood pouring out he said in Shawnee: "I was the border man's friend. Many times I have saved him and his people from harm. I never warred with you, but only to protect our wigwams and lands. I refused to join your paleface enemies with the red coats. I came to the fort as your friend and you murdered me. You have murdered by my side, my young son…For this, may the curse of the Great Spirit rest upon this land. May it be blighted by nature. May it even be blighted in its hopes. May the strength of its peoples be paralyzed by the stain of our blood."

Cornstalk spoke his last and gave up the ghost.

By now Captain Arbuckle arrived on the scene, looked around and said, "Damn, Damn, we will have hell to pay now!"

Captain Arbuckle gave orders for the mob to clean up the mess and take the Indians out and bury them. They took Cornstalk and buried him in front of the fort facing both the Ohio and Kanawha Rivers, but they carried Red Hawk, Elinipsico, and the brave to the bank of the Kanawha River and rolled them into the water never to be seen again in this age. Elinipsico left four orphans; most of Red Hawk's and Cornstalk's children were grown.

Has Cornstalk's Curse Come True?

Could the freak lightning strikes have been caused by Cornstalk's curse?

Many tragedies and disasters were blamed on the curse:

The worst coal mine disaster in American history took place in Monongah, West Virginia on December 6, 1907 when 310 miners were killed.

In June 1944, 150 people were killed when a tornado ripped through the tri-state triangular area.

The devastating Silver Bridge disaster sent 46 people hurtling to their death in the Ohio River on December 15, 1967. Many have also connected this tragedy to the eerie sightings of the Mothman, strange lights in the sky, and odd paranormal happenings.

On November 14, 1970 a Southern Airways DC-10 crashed into a mountain near Huntington, West Virginia, killing 75 people on board.

In March 1976 of that year, the town of Point Pleasant was rocked in the middle of the night be an explosion at the Mason County Jail. Housed in the jail was a woman named Harriet Sisk, who had been arrested for the murder of her infant daughter. On March 2, her husband came to the jail with a suitcase full of explosives to kill himself and his wife and to destroy the building. Both of the Sisk's were killed, along with three law enforcement officers.

In January, 1978 a freight train derailed at Point Pleasant and dumped thousands of gallons of toxic chemicals. The chemicals contaminated the town's water supply and the wells had to be abandoned.

In April 1978 of that same year, the town of St. Mary's (north of Point Pleasant) was struck with tragedy when 51 men who were working on the Willow Island power plant were killed when their construction scaffolding collapsed.

And there have been many other strange occurrences, fires and floods. Most would say however that floods are a natural part of living on the river, although Point Pleasant was almost totally destroyed in 1913 and 1937. It might be hard to tie such natural occurrences into a curse, but what about the barge explosion that killed six men from town just before Christmas 1953? Or the fire that destroyed an entire downtown city block in the late 1880's?

Was it Cornstalks curse that brought this about?

David Crockett Whitt

sees Spirits

David Crockett Whitt is my Great Grandfather and a member of Company "H", of the Twenty-ninth Virginia Infantry. Source: The book, "Legacy, The Days Of David Crockett Whitt"

General Lee's army was tired and worn. They had fought Grant's people in the Battle of the Wilderness to a standstill while being out numbered six to ten. The fighting had shifted from the Wilderness to Spotsylvania County, where desperate actions had taken place. The Confederate's held a battle line along the North Anna River, now Pickett's division rejoined the Army of Northern Virginia. Crockett was familiar with this place because last summer the 29th marched through here and Hanover Junction. They only stayed four days then marched out on May 27th 1864. The line of defense moved to east of Richmond and just north of the Chickahominy River.

David Crockett Whitt a member of the Twenty-ninth Virginia Infantry arrived on this new front on May 30th and lost some more dear souls.

On May 31st the 29th Infantry moved two miles on the Confederate right and arrived at Cold Harbor on June 1st 1864.

The Confederate Army had built a zigzag breastwork which gave them a clear shot in a wide radius. The Confederates were out numbered a little less than two to one, but were well fortified. Actually General Lee hoped that Grant would send his boys that way. The heaviest fighting took place on June 3rd when Grant sent in a large number of soldiers trying to win by sheer numbers. It was an un-Godly slaughter as the Confederates mowed down seven thousand Union Boys in less than ten minutes. Neither side could believe their eyes as they saw a field of blue dead or wounded. The 29th was involved in this battle and were given the name of the "Bloody 29th".

The 29th did their duty but felt no honor this day as they saw the results of their action. Was General Grant this stupid, many of the men on both sides wondered?

It was reported that many of the Union boys wrote their name, address and a short testament as to their wishes after death, and pinned it inside their blouse before the charge.

Fighting went on in a lesser scale until June 13th, when the 29th Infantry was pulled out and marched to Melvin Hill near the James River.

Grant would not call a truce at Cold Harbor so that the wounded and dead could be removed. He thought it would declare a defeat for the North. It was sickening to see the bloated bodies that lay before them. Even wild hogs came out of the woods and dined on the dead and dying. The Confederates were not allowed to leave their breastworks for several days even to take care of bodily functions. It was a stinking mess in the trench and also in the field of view before them was horrifying.

Crockett was so shocked at this battle he would never forget it the rest of his life. The night of June 3rd many sounds came from the killing field as the wounded men begged for help. This is the stuff of life long nightmares.

Crockett saw many spirits rising from the dead as they released their souls.

The Spirits had a ghostly yellowish glow as they rose from the bodies on the Killing field.

He prayed most of the night. The Confederates lost fifteen hundred men in this conflict which was insignificant compared to the Union loss of seven thousand in a ten minute period.

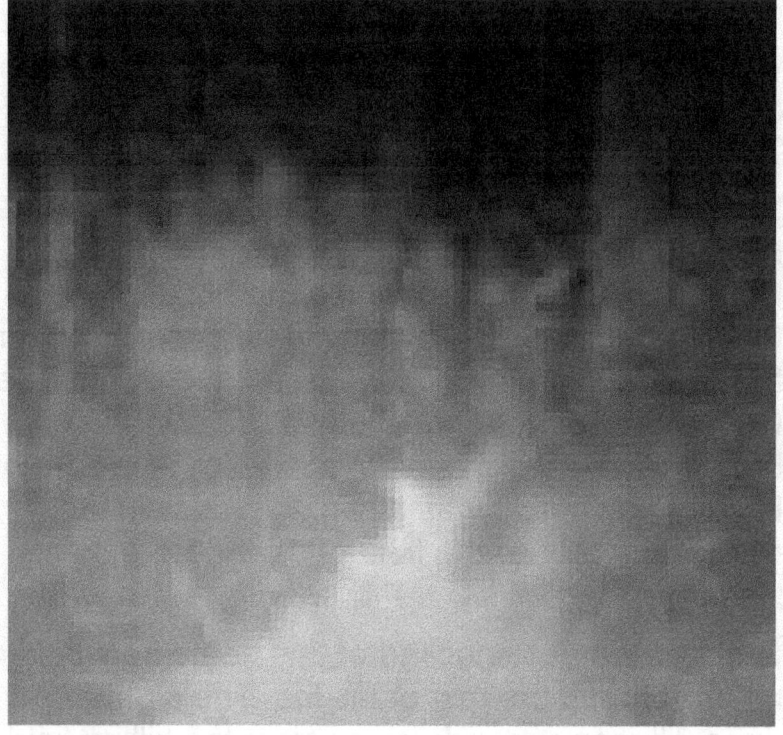

Spirits of Soldiers rising after the Battle of Cold Harbor. Think what you will!

Haunts of the Cold Harbor Battlefield

It was a foot race and this time won by General Lee and the Army of Northern Virginia. The Confederates had reached Cold Harbor first and immediately started digging in ready for the inevitable assault. General Grant and the Union Army was pushing towards Richmond and licking their wounds after the Battle of the Wilderness.

The Confederate line would reach nearly 7 miles when done with Cold Harbor in the center. The soldiers used bayonets, coffee cups, shovels, knives and even cut open canteens to build the earthworks that could save their lives. When Grants army arrived, they dug in just opposite of the Confederates at Cold Harbor the lines were a mere 300 yards apart.

General Lee had only one choice with Richmond only ten miles away, repel any Union attack at all cost. General Grant was eager, maybe too eager to crush Lee's army and end the war; he ordered an all out frontal attack across terrain that neither he nor any of his officers knew anything about. The result was a massacre of epic proportions.

Union soldiers, well aware of their fate, wrote their names on pieces of paper and fastened them to their uniforms hoping that it would be easier to identify them later. On June 3, 1864 at 4:30am, the charged was ordered. Union soldiers ran across an open field, Estimates are that 7,000 were killed or wounded in the first 30 minutes. All told the Union lost 13,000 men compared to 1,700 Confederates.

According to a Union survivor, *"Southern riflemen opened fire with one, long rolling volley– A sheet of flame, sudden as lightning, red as blood, and so near; it seemed to singe the men's faces."*

Lt. Colonel Charles Morgan said of the thousands lying in the blistering sun of June in Virginia, *"Vain calls for relief smote upon the ears of their comrades at every lull in the firing."*

It wasn't till later in his memoirs that Grant proclaimed that this was the charge he wished he never ordered. It was after this sound defeat that Grant stole away in the middle of the night and headed towards Petersburg.

Today the locals living in the area claim the battle still rages. Sounds of men screaming, gun fire, and cannon fire are often reported to the local papers. Pictures of soldiers and strange anomalies are plentiful as well as seeing apparitions of Union soldiers on the battlefield. Visitors to the park claim an overpowering smell of gun powder and unexplainable guile.

Bodies being cared for long after the battle of Cold Harbor by Union Negro soldiers.

Many odd happenings have occurred around Battle fields.

A body left from the carnage of the Battle of Gettysburg.

What do you think of this Eerie Couple?
The picture is thought to be the spirit of "Leck" Whitt and wife;
He was shot dead in the Court Yard at Magoffin County, KY.

Ghost stories from haunted Gettysburg

With 53,000 casualties in three days, if there is any place in America that would be susceptible to spirits remaining, it would be Gettysburg.

If it is at all possible, many believers in the supernatural end up visiting Gettysburg at some point in time or another. Thousands upon thousands of casualties (killed, wounded, and missing) fell on these fields during the first three days of July in 1863. Many were very young, some already married with families, and all were Americans. For those believing that any part of a spirit can be left behind, it is not difficult to see why Gettysburg would be the quintessential place it could happen.

Stories of ghostly sightings abound in this relatively small town in Pennsylvania. Gettysburg is situated just a few miles from the Maryland and Pennsylvania border, thus the Mason Dixon line. General Lee had crossed the border into the north and thousands of men and boys never saw home again after those three bloody days.

Over the years, certain ghost stories have stood out as the most poignant, memorable, or "famous." It might surprise many people to know that very few of the ghost stories of Gettysburg seem to be of the "scary" variety. A great number of people who witness apparitions here often mention that there was not a feeling of bad or evil in the incident, only sadness or a feeling of something unfinished.

There is one reported haunted site that does not have a direct tie to a soldier. The only civilian killed in the battle was "Jennie" Wade. Twenty year old Jennie was baking loaves of bread for the Union soldiers and was caught in the cross-fire. The home in which she fell still stands and offers tours. Often in the basement, where Jennie's body was taken by soldiers, visitors experience their paranormal encounter, but the entire house has had activity reported. No one knows exactly what spirits still reside in this house. Is it Jennie herself? Some have felt her father's presence. He was not with Jennie during the battle, is he remorseful for not being there when his daughter most needed him?

A short distance outside of town is the location of Sachs Bridge. This is one site where anyone wanting to capture ghostly images on camera film usually can do so. The beautiful bridge was built in the mid 1800s and both Union and Confederate troops used the bridge in 1863. The legend is that three Confederate soldiers were hung at this site, and some of the dead soldiers from the battle, the story goes, are still believed to have this soil as their final resting place. Are they trying to tell someone they should be resting in southern soil?

Devil's Den is another hot spot at which many sightings have taken place. Near the base of Little Round Top, this spot saw much intense fighting on the second day of the battle. Does something seem to linger here, as with many other places on the battlefield? Many people, supernatural believers or not, have admitted *"feeling something"* here and at the site of Pickett's Charge.

Other areas near Devil's Den that have offered encounters to ghost hunters are Triangular Field, the Valley of Death, the Wheatfield, the Peach Orchard, and the Slaughter Pen. This entire part of the battlefield saw so much suffering that whatever remains seems to be reaching out for some kind of comfort or closure.

Visitors to Spangler's Spring near Culp's Hill just may be lucky enough to catch a glimpse of "The Woman in White." The odd factor in this particular ghost story is that it is not necessarily battle related. The lady who is said to haunt this part of the battlefield is reported to have committed suicide after a love affair turned sour. Is she still waiting for promises to be filled?

Day three of the Battle of Gettysburg was one of

the deadliest in U. S. war history. Confederate soldiers numbering more than twelve thousand were ordered to march across an open field directly into the fire of the Union troops. They kept marching and they kept falling. The casualty numbers were immense and devastating, some reports setting the percentages at more than 50%. If there is one particular site in Gettysburg at which spirits remain to roam, this area, the site of Pickett's Charge, would be the location.

Although it has been said that a majority of paranormal experiences involve only the senses of smelling or hearing, this detail seems to be disproved when speaking with people who have had experiences at Gettysburg. A great number of paranormal reports from the battlefield seem to involve seeing soldiers in the blue or the gray. They are sometimes seen in a fog or mist and sometimes standing there just as plain as a traveling companion. Frequently it is indeed a smell or sound that is reported. Sounds of the battle are heard, cries of the wounded, the dying, the commands to run, hit the ground, or fire.

The spirits that may remain after the bloodbath that occurred on this rich Pennsylvania farmland of 1863 cannot be pinpointed to one area. Those looking to research Gettysburg and the battle need only to follow the maps for the battleground areas. From Reynolds Woods to Cemetery Hill to East Cavalry Field and finally ending at the National Cemetery, there have been sightings. Cameras have picked up ghost sightings all over town and all over the battlefield with the photographer usually oblivious to what is near enough to reach out and touch.

The college in town has its own famous ghost, *"Blue Boy."* There is a reportedly haunted orphanage in Gettysburg where sounds of the crying children are still heard. There is a photography studio said to be haunted that was a private home in 1863. It was the George House then and is where General Reynolds' body was taken after he was mortally wounded.

Hotels have resident ghost stories, there are nightly ghost walks, and even some of the countless monuments that cover the field have ghost sightings attached to them. Some of the locals are happy to talk about the subject; others try to convince visitors that there is nothing to prove the legends or sightings.

The bottom line is that a place at which so many

people died violently in a very short time is filled with ghost stories, whether real or legend. If you are planning a ghost-hunting expedition to Gettysburg, be sure to thoroughly research the history and lore of the area to assure full enjoyment of your visit.

Haunts at Point Lookout POW PEN

My Great Grandfather, David Crockett Whitt, survived this hell on earth from April 6, 1865 to June 22, 1865 as a POW in Point Lookout, Maryland. (Read about it in the book, "Legacy, The Days of David Crockett Whitt.")

Source: Dorcas Coleman

A figure appears ahead of you on the edge of a clearing. It is of a man, bearded, ragged and gaunt. As he draws nearer, you can see that his cheeks are sunken and eyes hollowed, giving the impression they might rattle around in his head like marbles in a box. His clothes, what's left of them, appear to be homespun, of wool, too heavy to be the type normally worn on a warm late summer day. He wears boots, dusty, the leather cracked, and his gait is loose, as if he has been walking for a long time. A canteen is slung across his shoulder. A belt that would normally sit at the waist hangs precariously from sharply angled hips. You find yourself staring and expect to make eye contact as he passes, but he continues to look straight ahead, seemingly oblivious to your presence. As he passes, you catch a whiff of musty, humus scent intermingled with gunpowder.

Though unfriendly, you are impressed by the accuracy and intensity of what you assume to be a historical re-enactor. A few steps later, you turn to take another look, but he's gone, vanished. You stop and listen, but there is no sound, other than the twittering of birds in the trees and your own breath. There is no one there. You feel the blood rush out of your head and your heart starts to race. You think you may have seen a ghost. If you're in <u>Point Lookout State Park</u>, chances are you have.

Whether you believe in ghosts, apparitions and poltergeists or not, the fact that Maryland's public lands have experienced more than their fair share of tragedy and unexplained phenomena is undisputable.

 Point Lookout State Park, located at the southernmost tip of Maryland's western shore, undoubtedly has the most grisly history of any of the state's parks.

Spectacularly lovely, Point Lookout sits on a

peninsula at the confluence of the Potomac River and the Chesapeake Bay. Today its completely serene panorama consists of lovely stretches of beach and dense stands of loblolly pine. But this was not always the case. While it seems hard to believe today, Point Lookout State Park was once the site of the Civil War's largest prison camp.

The tolls of war

Point Lookout began as part of St. Michael's Manor; one of three manors owned by Leonard Calvert, the first Governor of the Maryland colony. In the 200 years leading up to the Civil War, it became a popular summer resort, complete with beach cottages, a large wharf and a lighthouse. With the advent of the war, people's attentions turned away from recreation and the area's summer resort owners began to suffer financially.

The U.S. Government, needing a hospital to house casualties of the Northern armies, leased the Point Lookout resort; Hammond General Hospital was built and received its first Union Army patients on August 17, 1862. Early in 1863, the authorities ordered a small number of Confederate prisoners confined to the hospital grounds, most being Southern Marylanders accused of helping the Confederacy. Not long after the Battle of Gettysburg, the federal government expanded the hospital's grounds and built a prison camp for Confederate soldiers. Point Lookout was close to the battlefields yet isolated enough to make escape difficult. The site became officially known as Camp Hoffman, a rebel camp capable of holding 10,000 prisoners of war. Three forts were erected to protect the prison, one of which, Fort Lincoln, still remains. As the war progressed, additional prisoners were assigned to Camp Hoffman. In September 1863,

4,000 Confederates were being held at the camp; by December the number had more than doubled to 9,000. By the following June, less than one year after the camp more than 20,000 prisoners crowded the camp.

Point Lookout was used mainly for enlisted men, but most officers were sent to Fort Delaware. During the prison's operation, filth prevailed and wells became contaminated. Men literally froze to death in Sibley tents, rudimentary structures offering little protection from the elements, with but one blanket apiece and very little wood. With money scarce and boredom plentiful, the prisoners learned to occupy themselves making trinkets and many other useful articles out of various materials that were subsequently used for bartering purposes.

At the end of the Civil War in April 1865, Federal officials began transferring the Confederates south; (They had to take the "Oath," and were given train passage, but many of the southern rail roads were out.) by late June the last prisoners were gone. In just under two years, out of 52,264 Confederates imprisoned at Point Lookout, between 3,000 and 8,000 men died.

Today, two monuments honor the memory of the

prisoners who died there. The first was built by the State of Maryland and dedicated in 1876. The U.S. Government followed suit, erecting the second monument in the early 1900s. In 1965, 100 years following the end of the Civil War, the Maryland State Forest & Park Service began development of Point Lookout State Park. Today the park comprises 1,064 acres.
Let there be light.

One of the most well known and reputedly haunted sites at the park, the Point Lookout Lighthouse, still stands. No longer in use, the lighthouse first came into existence in 1830 as a one-and-a-half story wooden and masonry building. In 1883 another story was added to house two keepers and their families, allowing the arduous duties involved in lighthouse keeping to be shared.

Keepers of previous generations did not enjoy the advantages of automatic alarm systems to alert them if the light went out or mechanical means for ringing the fog bells. If weather was foggy for a week, the bell had to sound constantly, so the whole family had to take turns ringing.

Point Lookout's lighthouse was active for more

than 135 years until the Navy purchased it in 1965, after which an automated light was placed offshore. It remained tenanted until 1981.
Who goes there?

Over the decades, there have been numerous reports of paranormal experiences within Point Lookout State Park, but none more so than in the lighthouse itself. These reports eventually reached the ears of the internationally-renowned parapsychologist, Dr. Hans Holzer, along with his team of paranormal psychologists, was the first to investigate the lighthouse some 20 years ago. To this day it remains the only Chesapeake Bay lighthouse to have earned such esteemed scrutiny.

Holzer's team successfully recorded 24 different voices in the building, both male and female, Voices singing and talking often using quite colorful language. One comment, *"Fire if they get too close to you,"* was thought to reference the great number of Confederate soldiers imprisoned nearby. A female voice recorded on the tower staircase and believed to be that of Ann Davis, wife of the first keeper spoke of *"my home."* Yet another voice said, *"Let us not take objection to what they are doing."*

Lighthouse visitors, including Dr. Holzer's team, have experienced very chilly air in parts of the building, along with a rotten smell emanating from one particular room. Oddly, as soon as Dr. Holzer made public his belief that the smell was from the tormented spirits of people held there against their will, those falsely accused of spying or having Confederate sympathies -- the smell disappeared.

In addition to unusual sounds and smells, many spectral visions have also been reported, such as that of Ann Davis, standing at the top of the stairs in a white blouse and long blue skirt.

Several unexplained images have appeared in photographs, the most well known being that of *"The Ghost of Point Lookout,"* taken during a séance in the lighthouse in the late 70s. In the photograph, Laura Berg, a former lighthouse resident, stands in the center holding a candle. To her left, the foggy form of a man in soldier garb, weapon, sash, one leg casually crossed over the other, appears to be leaning into the wall. Interestingly, this image was not noticed by those attending the séance; it was seen only later, in the photo.

An eyewitness reports

Need more evidence? Consider the following tales related by *Ranger Donnie Hammett, longtime manager of Point Lookout State Park, as he personally experienced them.*

An initial encounter

The incident I am about to relate occurred on an unseasonably warm day in early March of 1977. I had been a park ranger at Point Lookout for only two months. Although mine was a new job, Point

Lookout was not new to me. I had lived my lifetime of 25 years in the Point Lookout area. I was working the evening shift. It was a weekday and despite the beautiful, warm weather there were few park visitors.

At about 4:30 pm, I was on the Potomac River beachfront gathering and recording weather data when I noticed an elderly woman standing about 40 yards from me. She caught my attention because she was strangely shuffling along, looking toward her feet. She appeared to be desperately looking for something she had lost in the grass.

After I had watched her for about five minutes, I walked over to offer my assistance. My first thought was that perhaps she had lost her keys. She seemed very distant and our conversation was very brief. I only remember three points she made: she did not need my assistance, she lived up the beach "a ways," and she asked if I knew where the gravestones were that used to be where we were standing.

I remember that for some reason I felt I was imposing on the woman and not wanting to be an imposition, I left to walk 300 yards east to the Chesapeake Bay shore to record more data.

About five minutes later, while I was walking back to my truck which I had left parked near the River, I noticed that the woman had disappeared. It was then that I realized the adjacent parking lot was empty. Furthermore, from my vantage point since our conversation, I would have had to have seen any cars entering or leaving the area. None had. I did not conduct a search for the woman though I often wish I had done so.

A few hours later I asked then park manager, Gerry Sword, if he knew anything about a graveyard near the Potomac River picnic area. He wanted to know why I was asking, so I told him about my odd encounter with the old woman.

After Mr. Sword heard my story, he told me that there had once been a graveyard somewhere near where the mysterious lady had been wandering. It was the Taylor family graveyard. Its exact location is no longer known, but its former existence is well documented. Records show that one of the individuals buried in the lost graveyard is Elizabeth Taylor. Evidently someone had come across the missing burial site and stolen her headstone. Elizabeth Taylor's grave marker was found in a local hotel by a Point Lookout park ranger.

Some years later my mother, Regina Hammett, and I went to the site where I had talked to the old woman. We searched for signs of a graveyard using metal rods to probe down through the sand. Within minutes we located a rectangular, rocklike form under about a foot of sand. Soon we located several other possible gravestones laid out in regular rows as one would expect. However when we dug up a couple of these objects, we discovered they were concrete foundations of a 1860s Civil War warehouse. The Taylor family cemetery has never been found.

Could the strange woman have been the deceased Elizabeth Taylor searching for the rest of her family?

More sightings

On several occasions, I have witnessed a man running across the road through Point Lookout. The sightings always took place during the day, on the same section of road, and the man always crossed the road just after my truck had passed, causing me to view him in my rearview mirror.

The man was always crossing in the same direction. Other rangers have experienced the same phenomenon while passing in other vehicles at different times of the day and different times of the year.

The first time I saw the man I immediately returned to the crossing site. The man was running, using long strides. He first appeared at the edge of the road adjacent to one of the Point Lookout camping areas. He crossed the road and dashed into the woods on the other side, leaving park property. My first thought was that he was a trespasser fleeing the area. I examined the area but was unable to find any type of path on either side of the road or any evidence of human or animal crossing. I did not get a good enough look at the intruder to identify him or describe his attire.

The site of the man's crossing is very near but not in the original Confederate soldier cemetery... used to bury prisoners who had died of smallpox at the nearby smallpox hospital where sick Confederates were held. Had the man been making the same trek during the Civil War, he would have been running in a route taking him directly away from the smallpox hospital. Reportedly, Confederate prisoners would trick their Union guards into sending them to the hospital and then would attempt an escape through the same woods from which I had seen the man flee. Could the figure have been the spirit of a Confederate prisoner who escaped from the smallpox hospital, only to die in the nearby woods, having himself been infected with the deadly disease as often happened?

Powerful currents

Power outages are not at all unusual at Point Lookout. Being located on a peninsula, electricity can only be brought in from one direction. If those lines are interrupted the Point is left in darkness. Because of this, Point Lookout residents always keep candles and matches available.

One dark and stormy night when the power was out on the Point, Gerry Sword experienced something we have yet to explain.

According to Mr. Sword, he lit three identical candles in a candelabrum in the living room. Mr. Sword left the candelabra for a short time to go to the kitchen to fix dinner. A few minutes later he heard a loud sound come from the room where he had left the candelabra unattended. Being alone in the house, he immediately went to investigate the disturbance. The candelabrum was as he had left it only now there was a marked difference in the size of the candles. One had only burned about an inch; the second had burned nearly four inches. But it was the third candle that is hardest to explain. Only about an inch of this candle remained, however a section of the candle rested on the floor nearby. Apparently, somehow the candle had been broken. The wick on the length of candle lying on the floor had been lit, but now was extinguished. Inexplicably, the small piece of candle in the candelabra was aflame.

A sixth sense

It is said that dogs can perceive things humans cannot. They can hear things the human ear can't and their superior sense of smell is well known. Perhaps dogs have other senses completely alien to us, senses we could not understand.

Later Mr. Sword moved to a property located adjacent to an old Civil War road that ran the length of Point Lookout. On several occasions, Mr. Sword's German Shepard seemed to "see" someone or something traveling on the old Civil War road. Sometimes the dog would sit and he watched the invisible traffic go by for long periods of time. Other times the dog would bark and lunge against its chain, as if trying to get at an intruder walking down the road, though none was ever seen. I have noticed my dogs stare down the hall at nothing, or is there something that only they can see?

More Eerie Tales

Following is a series of encounters experienced and told by Laura Berg, former resident of the Lookout Lighthouse.
Just passing through

Before moving into the lighthouse, Ms. Berg learned of the strange things that happened to the former park manager, Gerry Sword, during the time he lived there. Mr. Sword frequently heard snoring in the kitchen. At times he would hear voices outside of the back of the house but when he checked, there was no one there. Then he would hear voices in the front yard and again upon checking, there was no one to be found.

This happened frequently. One evening he actually saw figures of men going through the house! Ms. Berg also learned that numerous fishermen throughout the years had heard calls

for help on the water only to discover that there was no one to be found.
In the company of strangers

The first night Ms. Berg spent in the lighthouse; she was awakened to the sound of heavy or old-fashioned boots walking up and down the hall. She also relayed that one of the rooms had a very bad odor at night. Some mornings she heard a female voice at the top of the stairs singing. She never could tell what song it was, but it seemed to be a very happy one. Sometimes she heard the sound of men laughing and talking in the south-side living room and whenever she checked for intruders, she never found anyone. She only actually saw something one time, two figures in the basement. They were transparent and Ms. Berg couldn't tell if they were male or female.

Coming to call

Ms. Berg enjoyed family and friends visiting her in the lighthouse. Several of them had strange experiences. One time when her parents were visiting her from Baltimore her mother was awakened in the middle of the night by someone calling her name, Helen.

Another friend who was visiting her went into the living room alone and saw a woman in a blue dress. Thinking it was another guest, she went to ask Ms. Berg who it was. Both of them returned to the living room, but no one was there.

A guardian angel?

Ms. Berg's most vivid memory was being awakened one night and seeing an unusual series of six lights. She thought it might have been a reflection from a boat or a car, but when she looked out all was dark. As she became more awake she suddenly smelled smoke. She jumped up and raced downstairs and found her space heater on fire. She was able to put the fire out but the entire wire was burnt, as was the wall socket. She realized that if she hadn't been awakened by the lights the whole house could have burned, with her in it. She felt like someone was looking out for her and that she was safe.

Through the time that Laura Berg spent in the lighthouse she had many strange experiences but she never felt threatened.

These are only a few of the many unexplained

phenomenon, people have experienced while visiting the park. Still not convinced? Perhaps a personal visit is in order.

Dorcas Coleman, assistant editor of The Natural Resource, is also a true believer in the spirits.

This engraving shows the final skirmish between forces on Cemetery Hill, at the Battle of Gettysburg.

Lincoln Giving the Gettysburg Address

More Ghost of the Civil War

Source: Wikipedia, the free encyclopedia

There is speculation over the alleged existence of **ghosts** from the **American Civil War**. Among the locales famous for Civil War ghosts was the Sharpsburg battlefield near Sharpsburg, Maryland, Chickamauga battlefield outside Chattanooga, Tennessee across the Georgia border, Harper's Ferry, West Virginia, Buras, Louisiana, and Warren, Arkansas.

More Gettysburg

The Battle of Gettysburg was the largest battle in North America. Fittingly, it has many ghost stories. The 20th Maine was said to have seen the ghost of George Washington, and it was due to the ghost that they found their way to the Gettysburg battlefield. The Soldiers' Orphanage cellar is said to make even psychics too afraid to enter the house, due to its legend. The Herr Tavern was built in 1815, but during the battle it was used as the first Confederate hospital at Gettysburg, where amputations often resulted in limbs being thrown out through the window to be collected later, only for many of the soldiers to die afterward. As a result, four of the guest rooms are said to be haunted and the rooms are numbered so that there is no room 13.

The interest of ghosts and Gettysburg remains to the present day. In recent times, people have claimed to seen ghost soldiers and sometimes even ghost battles, in many places around Gettysburg, Pennsylvania. Eight separate companies offer ghost tours in Gettysburg, some seasonally, and some all year.

Other battlefields

A battle did not need to be major to have ghosts associated with it. The Battle of Kolb Farm is believed to have created a ghost that haunts a farmhouse in northern Georgia.

One of the bloodiest battles was the Battle of Sharpsburg. Both Union and Confederate Ghosts have reportedly been seen placing artillery on the battlefield.

Willie Lincoln, who died in the White House during his father's presidency.

Lincoln's Ghost

Abraham Lincoln has long been said to haunt the White House. First Lady Grace Coolidge, wife of President Calvin Coolidge, was the first to claim to spot Lincoln's ghost. She claimed to see Lincoln looking at the Potomac River sadly from the Oval Office. Carl Sandburg claimed to have "sensed" Lincoln do the same as well. Both Queen Wilhelmina of the Netherlands and Eleanor Roosevelt were said to have seen Lincoln during World War II at the Lincoln Bedroom (Lincoln's office during the war). The Queen admitted to fainting after seeing Lincoln in his top hat. Margaret Truman's hearing of tappings that caused Harry Truman to order the White House renovated, keeping the building from falling down, have been attributed to the ghost. Gerald Ford's daughter Susan Ford made a point of never sleeping in the Lincoln Bedroom, out of fear of Lincoln's ghost. Maureen Reagan claimed to see Lincoln in the Lincoln Bedroom as well during her father's (Ronald Reagan) administration. Others who have sensed or reportedly seen Lincoln was Harry Truman.

Lincoln's son Willie died during Lincoln's Presidency. A White House maid during Ulysses

S. Grant's administration reported seeing the dead boy.

Lincoln's ghost has reportedly been seen outside of the White House as well. In Loundonville, New York, Lincoln's ghost is said to haunt a house that was owned by a woman who was present at Ford's Theatre when Lincoln was shot by John Wilkes Booth. Other Lincoln hauntings include his grave in Springfield, Illinois, a portrait of Mary Todd Lincoln, and a phantom train on nights in April along the same path his funeral train followed from Washington D.C. to Springfield.

Ghosts of Antietam Battlefield and the Bloody Lane

Source: Rickie Longfellow

The bloodiest battle of the Civil War took place on September 17, 1862, on Antietam Creek near the small town of Sharpsburg, Maryland. Four hours of intense fighting took place on an old sunken road that separated two farms. A staggering 23,100 men were wounded, killed or missing in action after the Union and Confederate Armies collided in the nearby cornfields, farmlands and Antietam Creek.

When the Confederate Army reached the sunken road, which provided some protection at first, General Robert E. Lee ordered that the battle be held there. Soldiers on both sides fired continuously as the Federals tried repeatedly to overtake the position. Finally, the Confederate soldiers were overrun and bodies fell on top of bodies in the bloodied sunken road.

Today we know it as Bloody Lane and if you ever have occasion to walk it you will indeed go back in time and be humbled by the experience. The tragic impressions of that day seem to linger. It seems that no matter how many visitors roam the old road on any given day, it remains church-like quiet.

The Sunken Road- later renamed the Bloody Lane, where more than 5,000 died.

According to eyewitnesses, Bloody Lane is haunted. Gunfire and the smell of gunpowder have been reported when no one is on the road or even nearby. One visitor to the battlefield saw several men in Confederate uniforms walking Bloody Lane. He thought they were reenactors until they vanished. The most convincing of the reports is the one of some Baltimore schoolboys who walked Bloody Lane and heard singing out in the fields. They said it sounded like a chant or the Christmas song *Deck the Halls*. They heard a chant similar to Fa-la-la-la-la sound repeatedly. The area was near the observation tower where the Irish Brigade charged the Confederates with a battle cry in Gaelic, which sounded like the Christmas carol.

Another haunted area is Burnside's Bridge, known then as Rohrback Bridge, where General Ambrose Burnside pushed the Confederates back after many defeated attempts. Many soldiers were buried quickly in and around the bridge in unmarked graves. Visitors at night have reported seeing balls of blue light moving around the sound of drum playing cadence as it fades into the night. Perhaps the Battle of Antietam is not over for some restless spirits.

The Pry House and The Piper House stand on the battlefield. Both are reported to be haunted-

stories ranging from footsteps heard on the stairs
to apparitions of a woman thought to be the wife
of one of the generals who died in the house.

Photographs by Rickie Longfellow

The St. Paul Episcopal Church in Sharpsburg
was used as a Confederate hospital after the
battle. Reports tell of the screams of injured and
dying still coming from the building. Others report
seeing flickering lights from the church's tower.

The wounded were taken into nearby Sharpsburg
to the church and into people's homes to be
cared for and many of them died there after
surviving the horrendous battle. There is a house
west of the town of Mt. Airy where some of the
wounded were taken. Legend has it that the
floorboards in the house are still stained with
blood and cannot be removed even with sanding.

Abraham Lincoln at Antietam 1862

Ghosts of Andersonville

Andersonville August 17, 1864 Photographic Print - *Public Domain*

Eerie noises include gunshots, marching, voices talking and moaning. Specters of both armies have been sighted. There is an unearthly putrid stench.

Andersonville Prison was built during the Civil War to hold Union POWs. It is in Americus, Georgia. The prison was made of tents and huts hastily erected inside a blockade on 27 acres of land. It housed about thirty-two thousand prisoners.

It's thought that about thirteen thousand soldiers died there from starvation, dehydration, dysentery caused by stagnant water, being shot by guards during escape attempts or violence between prisoners. Today, as the Andersonville National Historic Site, it honors all American POWs.

Andersonville Horror

On February 27, 1864 this was called Camp Sumter/Andersonville Prison. The conditions were atrocious. Supplies were short and the facility was overcrowded. The South could barely feed the army, but the North had no excuse for the treatment at Point Lookout Prison.

There were violent gangs that prisoners had to contend with. The Raiders were one group of predatory Union soldiers who assaulted fellow prisoners and stole from them to survive.

Soon, they robbed for affluence and egoism. The regulators (Other Prisoners stepped up to make things right) were created to deal with them. They captured raiders and held trials. Six raiders were hanged while others endured lesser punishments.

Andersonville's "Henry" Wirz

The captain was a Swiss immigrant and former doctor. He was commander of Camp Sumter and the prison from March 1864, until the prison was shut down over a year later.

Wirz was captured by the Union within a month of the Confederacy's defeat and was tried for war crimes relating to the squalid conditions at Andersonville. He was hanged on November 10, 1865, the only person court marshaled, convicted and executed for war crimes during the Civil War. His apparition has been sighted. I wonder why the Commander of Point Lookout wasn't hanged also.

The Hauntings of Andersonville

The Andersonville prison is associated with an array of mysterious, paranormal activity.

There have been reports of various paranormal at the former prison.

Eerie noises including gunshots, marching, voices talking and moaning are heard.

There's a stench that people smell in the general area of the camp. It reminded one Vietnam veteran of the odor of a military field hospital.

Bill Blue and Currie McClellan visited the park. They went to the cemetery and looked at the graves of the executed raiders. They spit on the grave of the leader and damned him to hell. Then they slept in their van. A little after midnight, Currie awoke to a putrid stench. Soon, the odor woke Bill. Then, they heard ghostly voices shouting for Willie, the leader's name. The date was July 11, the anniversary of the raiders' executions.

Father Whelan, a Catholic priest, was one of the chaplains who did what he could to comfort the inmates. Years later, historian Robert Berry, who wrote about Andersonville in his master's thesis, was walking on the grounds during twilight. He saw a strange figure walking ahead of him. He smelled the putrid odor. The stranger vanished. Later, Berry heard a voice behind him say he was going to give him the last rites. When he turned, he saw Whelan's specter.

People have reported seeing dim figures in a mystic fog, accompanied by sounds of screaming.

Source: Jill Stefko

This old house belonged to Hezekiah Whitt. It was log underneath and stood from 1782 to 2004. Many deaths were recorded here over the years and Nancy Skaggs Whitt (Wife of James Whitt.) died in the backyard and was buried where she fell. There were many reports of strange things happening here and strange noises were heard.

I End this book with many strange reports of ghosts and historic actions of Native Americans.

I am only reporting what I have found and leave it up to you to decide if you believe in the "Super Natural." Do you believe the "Mystic stories of Indians living in coexistence with the Spirit World?" Reports were given of the many accounts of ghost on the battlefields.

What do you believe?

The Author

Colonel Charles Dahnmon Whitt Author Of:
"Legacy, The Days Of David Crockett Whitt", "The
Patriot, Hezekiah Whitt," and "Dahnmon's Little

Stories." Coming soon: "Confederate American" and "Haunts and Spirits of the Past.")

Whitt a native of Tazewell County, Virginia moved to Kentucky in 1970 to carry out his trade as a Sheet Metal Worker with Local 24, Southern Ohio. Although he is now retired, he has always had an interest in genealogy and was always a real history buff for regional and civil war history; however, he didn't pursue his interest until he started researching his ancestry on-line in 1999.

While tracing his family's heritage, Whitt was soon introduced to his great-grandfather David Crockett Whitt. Yes, the discoveries that he had made during his fascinating search led him to create "Legacy, The Days of David Crockett Whitt," a work of historical fiction with his great-grandfather serving as the skeleton for this account of life in an earlier, and harder time.

Legacy follows Whitt's great-grandfather "Crockett," through the early settler days in Virginia and Kentucky from 1836 thru 1909, his formative years in Greenup County Kentucky and the time that he spent in a Civil War prison. Other regional areas mentioned in this particular title include: Portsmouth, South Shore, Hanging Rock, Greenup, Pogue's Landing, Catlettsburg and Ironton. There are also five chapters included in this writing that are devoted to David Crockett Whitt's war records as well. The book covers some information about Pike, Floyd, Johnson, Lawrence, Greenup, Carter, and Boyd Counties in Kentucky. It covers the entire length of the Tug Fork, on the West Virginia side. The book includes Crockett's detailed service in the Company H, of 29th Virginia Infantry from April 1862 until captured in the evening of April 8, 1865. Much of the book takes in Tazewell and now Buchanan County, VA. Most of the names, dates, and all the places are accurate. Crockett comes alive as you read this 580 page hardback novel.

Haunts and Spirits of the Past

In Legacy, you will soon discover when acquainting yourself with this particular title is that Whitt encompasses his faith and shows this pioneer family relying on their faith as well to get through trying times.

Charles is able to use the prefix "Colonel" in his pen-name because he is a Kentucky Colonel.

To purchase his books go to http://dahnmonwhittfamily.com for a signed book, write to Post Office Box 831, Flatwoods, KY. 41139. Price for this researched 580 page hardback book is $30.00 plus $6.00 for shipping. Published and sold by Jesse Stuart Foundation in Ashland, Kentucky. My Phone # 606 836 7997   E-Mail c-dahnmon@roadrunner.com

Below is the grave of David Crockett Whitt

Spirits of the Dead

This is a collection of short stories and poems of my life's happenings. Humor, Seriousness, and Christian Witness. $10. plus $4. shipping.
Send check to Charles Whitt, Box 831, Flatwoods, Ky. 41139

Just Published!

This hardback covers the years 1760-1838 and is centered on Tazewell County. Indian stories abound. It list all know descendents of Hezekiah Whitt. Hezekiah was a Virginia Militiaman, Indian Spy, Sheriff, and a life long Justice Of The Peace of the new county of Tazewell. It is a preamble to the Legacy listed below. $30. plus $6. shipping. I will sign it for you.

Just Published!

Legacy deals with the years of 1836 to 1900 and is centered on Tazewell County. It covers some years in Greenup County, KY. It covers Crockett's Civil War Years with the 29th Virginia Infantry. You will laugh and cry as you travel with Crockett. Price $30. plus $6. shipping
Order all these fine books from Charles Whitt, Box 831, Flatwoods, KY. 41139. I sign every book I send out.

Published Dec. 2008

www.ingramcontent.com/pod-product-compliance
Lightning Source LLC
Chambersburg PA
CBHW072357190626
46811CB00019B/1206